Copenhagen

A Play in Two Acts

by Michael Frayn

A SAMUEL FRENCH ACTING EDITION

SAMUEL
FRENCH
FOUNDED 1830
New York Hollywood London Toronto
SAMUELFRENCH.COM

ISBN 978-0-573-62752-1   Printed in U.S.A.   #5809

IMPORTANT BILLING AND CREDIT REQUIREMENTS

All producers of COPENHAGEN *must* give credit to the Author of the Play in all programs distributed in connection with performances of the Play and in all instances in which the title of the Play appears for purposes of advertising, publicizing or otherwise exploiting the Play and/or a production. The name of the Author *must* also appear on a separate line, on which no other name appears, immediately following the title, and *must* appear in size of type not less than fifty percent the size of the title type.

COPENHAGEN
opened in London at the Cottesloe Theatre,
Royale National Theatre,
on May 28, 1998.

Cast:

MARGRETHE BOHR	Sara Kestelman
NIELS BOHR	David Burke
WERNER HEISENBERG	Mathew March

Directed by Michael Blakemore
Designed by Peter J. Davison
Lighting by Mark Henderson
Sound by Simon Baker

This production moved to the Duchess Theatre, London,
where it was presented by Michael Codron and Lee Dean,
and opened on February 5, 1999.

* * *

COPENHAGEN
opened in New York on Broadway at the Royal Theatre
on April 11, 2000.

Cast:

MARGRETHE BOHR	Blair Brown
NIELS BOHR	Phillip Bosco
WERNER HEISENBERG	Michael Cumpsty

Directed by Michael Blakemore
Designed by Peter J. Davison
Lighting by Mark Henderson *and* Michael Lincoln
Sound by Tony Meola

Winner of
2000 Tony Award: Best Broadway Play
Outer Circle Critics Award: Outstanding Broadway Play
New York Drama Critic's Award: Best Foreign Play

ACT ONE

MARGRETHE. But why?

BOHR. You're still thinking about it?

MARGRETHE. Why did he come to Copenhagen?

BOHR. Does it matter, my love, now we're all three of us dead and gone?

MARGRETHE. Some questions remain long after their owners have died. Lingering like ghosts. Looking for the answers they never found in life.

BOHR. Some questions have no answers to find.

MARGRETHE. Why did he come? What was he trying to tell you?

BOHR. He did explain later.

MARGRETHE. He explained over and over again. Each time he explained it became more obscure.

BOHR. It was probably very simple, when you come right down to it: he wanted to have a talk.

MARGRETHE. A talk? To the enemy? In the middle of a war?

BOHR. Margrethe, my love, we were scarcely the enemy.

MARGRETHE. It was 1941!

BOHR. Heisenberg was one of our oldest friends.

MARGRETHE. Heisenberg was German. We were Danes. We were under German occupation.

BOHR. It put us in a difficult position, certainly.

MARGRETHE. I've never seen you as angry with anyone as you were with Heisenberg that night.

BOHR. Not to disagree, but I believe I remained remarkably calm.

MARGRETHE. I know when you're angry.

BOHR. It was as difficult for him as it was for us.

MARGRETHE. So why did he do it? Now no one can be hurt, now no one can be betrayed.

BOHR. I doubt if he ever really knew himself.

MARGRETHE. And he wasn't a friend. Not after that visit. That was the end of the famous friendship between Niels Bohr and Werner Heisenberg.

HEISENBERG. Now we're all dead and gone, yes, and there are only two things the world remembers about me. One is the uncertainty principle, and the other is my mysterious visit to Niels Bohr in Copenhagen in 1941. Everyone understands uncertainty. Or thinks he does. No one understands my trip to Copenhagen. Time and time again I've explained it. To Bohr himself, and Margrethe. To interrogators and intelligence officers, to journalists and historians. The more I've explained, the deeper the uncertainty has become. Well, I shall be happy to make one more attempt. Now we're all dead and gone. Now no one can be hurt, now no one can be betrayed.

MARGRETHE. I never entirely liked him, you know. Perhaps I can say that to you now.

BOHR. Yes, you did. When he was first here in the twenties? Of course you did. On the beach at Tisvilde with us and the boys? He was one of the family.

MARGRETHE. Something alien about him, even then.

BOHR. So quick and eager.

MARGRETHE. Too quick. Too eager.

BOHR. Those bright watchful eyes.

MARGRETHE. Too bright. Too watchful.

BOHR. Well, he was a very great physicist. I never changed my mind about that.

MARGRETHE. They were all good, all the people who came to Copenhagen to work with you. You had most of the great pioneers in atomic theory here at one time or another.

BOHR. And the more I look back on it, the more I think Heisenberg was the greatest of them all.

HEISENBERG. So what was Bohr? He was the first of us all, the father of us all. Modern atomic physics began when Bohr realized that quantum theory applied to matter as well as to energy. 1913. Everything we did was based on that great insight of his.

BOHR. When you think that he first came here to work with me in 1924 ...

HEISENBERG. I'd only just finished my doctorate, and Bohr was the most famous atomic physicist in the world.

BOHR. ... and in just over a year he'd invented quantum mechanics.

MARGRETHE. It came out of his work with you.

BOHR. Mostly out of what he'd been doing with Max Born and Pascual Jordan at Göttingen. Another year or so and he'd got uncertainty.

MARGRETHE. And you'd done complementarity.

BOHR. We argued them both out together.

HEISENBERG. We did most of our best work together.

BOHR. Heisenberg usually led the way.

HEISENBERG. Bohr made sense of it all.

BOHR. We operated like a business.

HEISENBERG. Chairman and managing director.

MARGRETHE. Father and son.

HEISENBERG. A family business.

MARGRETHE. Even though we had sons of our own.

BOHR. And we went on working together long after he ceased to be my assistant.

HEISENBERG. Long after I'd left Copenhagen in 1927 and gone back to Germany. Long after I had a chair and a family of my own.

MARGRETHE. Then the Nazis came to power....

BOHR. And it got more and more difficult. When the war broke out - impossible. Until that day in 1941.

MARGRETHE. When it finished forever.

BOHR. Yes, why did he do it?

HEISENBERG. September, 1941. For years I had it down in my memory as October.

MARGRETHE. September. The end of September.

BOHR. A curious sort of diary memory is.

HEISENBERG. You open the pages, and all the neat headings and tidy jottings dissolve around you.

BOHR. You step through the pages into the months and days themselves.

MARGRETHE. The past becomes the present inside your head.

HEISENBERG. September, 1941, Copenhagen ... And at once - here I am, getting off the night train from Berlin with my colleague Carl von Weizsäcker. Two plain civilian suits and raincoats among all the field-grey Wehrmacht uniforms arriving with us, all the naval gold braid, all the well-tailored black of the SS. In my bag I have the text of the lecture I'm giving. In my head is another communication that has to be delivered. The lecture is on astrophysics. The text inside my head is a more difficult one.

BOHR. We obviously can't go to the lecture.

MARGRETHE. Not if he's giving it at the German Cultural Institute - it's a Nazi propaganda organization.

BOHR. He must know what we feel about that.

HEISENBERG. Weizsäcker has been my John the Baptist, and written to warn Bohr of my arrival.

MARGRETHE. He wants to see you?

BOHR. I assume that's why he's come.

HEISENBERG. But how can the actual meeting with Bohr be arranged?

MARGRETHE. He must have something remarkably important to say.

HEISENBERG. It has to seem natural. It has to be private.

MARGRETHE. You're not really thinking of inviting him to the house?

BOHR. That's obviously what he's hoping.

MARGRETHE. Niels! They've occupied our country!

BOHR. He is not they.

MARGRETHE. He's one of them.

HEISENBERG. First of all there's an official visit to Bohr's workplace, the Institute for Theoretical Physics, with an awkward lunch in the old familiar canteen. No chance to talk to Bohr, of course. Is he even present? There's Rozental ... Petersen, I think ... Christian Møller, almost certainly.... It's like being in a dream. You can never quite focus the precise details of the scene around you. At the head of the table - is that Bohr? I turn to look, and it's Bohr, it's Rozental, it's Møller, it's whoever I appoint to be there ... A difficult occasion, though - I remember that clearly enough.

BOHR. It was a disaster. He made a very bad impression. Occupation of Denmark unfortunate. Occupation of Poland, however, perfectly acceptable. Germany now certain to win the war.

HEISENBERG. Our tanks are almost at Moscow. What can stop us? Well, one thing, perhaps. One thing.

BOHR. He knows he's being watched, of course. One must remember that. He has to be careful about what he says.

MARGRETHE. Or he won't be allowed to travel abroad again.

BOHR. My love, the Gestapo planted microphones in his house. He told Goudsmit when he was in America. The SS brought him in for interrogation in the basement at the Prinz-Albrecht-Strasse.

MARGRETHE. And then they let him go again.

HEISENBERG. I wonder if they suspect for one moment how painful it was to get permission for this trip. The humiliating appeals to the Party, the demeaning efforts to have strings pulled by our friends in the Foreign Office.

MARGRETHE. How did he seem? Is he greatly changed?

BOHR. A little older.

MARGRETHE. I still think of him as a boy.

BOHR. He's nearly forty. A middle-aged professor, fast catching up with the rest of us.

MARGRETHE. You still want to invite him here?

BOHR. Let's add up the arguments on either side in a reasonably scientific way. Firstly, Heisenberg is a friend ...

MARGRETHE. Firstly, Heisenberg is a German.

BOHR. A White Jew. That's what the Nazis called him. He taught relativity, and they said it was Jewish physics. He couldn't mention Einstein by name, but he stuck with relativity, in spite of the most terrible attacks.

MARGRETHE. All the real Jews have lost their jobs. He's still teaching.

BOHR. He's still teaching relativity.

MARGRETHE. Still a professor at Leipzig.

BOHR. At Leipzig, yes. Not at Munich. They kept him out of the chair at Munich.

MARGRETHE. He could have been at Columbia.

BOHR. Or Chicago. He had offers from both.

MARGRETHE. He wouldn't leave Germany.

BOHR. He wants to be there to rebuild German science when Hitler goes. He told Goudsmit.

MARGRETHE. And if he's being watched it will all be reported upon. Who he sees. What he says to them. What they say to him.

HEISENBERG. I carry my surveillance around like an infectious disease. But then I happen to know that Bohr is also under surveillance.

MARGRETHE. And you know you're being watched yourself.

BOHR. By the Gestapo?

HEISENBERG. Does he realize?

BOHR. I've nothing to hide.

MARGRETHE. By our fellow-Danes. It would be a terrible betrayal of all their trust in you if they thought you were collaborating.

BOHR. Inviting an old friend to dinner is hardly collaborating.

MARGRETHE. It might appear to be collaborating.

BOHR. Yes. He's put us in a difficult position.

MARGRETHE. I shall never forgive him.

BOHR. He must have good reason. He must have very good reason.

HEISENBERG. This is going to be a deeply awkward occasion.

MARGRETHE. You won't talk about politics?

BOHR. We'll stick to physics. I assume it's physics he wants to talk to me about.

MARGRETHE. I think you must also assume that you and I aren't the only people who hear what's said in this house. If you want to speak privately you'd better go out in the open air.

BOHR. I shan't want to speak privately.

MARGRETHE. You could go for another of your walks together.

HEISENBERG. Shall I be able to suggest a walk?

BOHR. I don't think we shall be going for any walks. Whatever he has to say he can say where everyone can hear it.

MARGRETHE. Some new idea he wants to try out on you, perhaps.

BOHR. What can it be, though? Where are we off to next?

MARGRETHE. So now of course your curiosity's aroused, in spite of everything.

HEISENBERG. So now here I am, walking out through the autumn twilight to the Bohrs' house at Ny-Carlsberg. Followed, presumably, by my invisible shadow. What am I feeling? Fear, certainly - the touch of fear that one always feels for a teacher, for an employer, for a parent. Much worse fear about what I have to say. About how to express it. How to broach it in the first place. Worse fear still about what happens if I fail.

MARGRETHE. It's not something to do with the war?

BOHR. Heisenberg is a theoretical physicist. I don't think anyone has yet discovered a way you can use theoretical physics to kill people.

MARGRETHE. It couldn't be something about fission?

BOHR. Fission? Why would he want to talk to me about fission?

MARGRETHE. Because you're working on it.

BOHR. Heisenberg isn't.

MARGRETHE. Isn't he? Everybody else in the world seems to be. And you're the acknowledged authority.

BOHR. He hasn't published on fission.

MARGRETHE. It was Heisenberg who did all the original work on the physics of the nucleus. And he consulted you then, he consulted you at every step.

BOHR. That was back in 1932. Fission's only been around for the last three years.

MARGRETHE. But if the Germans were developing some kind of weapon based on nuclear fission ...

BOHR. My love, no one is going to develop a weapon based on nuclear fission.

MARGRETHE. But if the Germans were trying to, Heisenberg would be involved.

BOHR. There's no shortage of good German physicists.

MARGRETHE. There's no shortage of good German physicists in America or Britain.

BOHR. The Jews have gone, obviously.

HEISENBERG. Einstein, Wolfgang Pauli, Max Born ... Otto Frisch, Lise Meitner.... We led the world in theoretical physics! Once.

MARGRETHE. So who is there still working in Germany?

BOHR. Sommerfeld, of course. Von Laue.

MARGRETHE. Old men.

BOHR. Wirtz. Harteck.

MARGRETHE. Heisenberg is head and shoulders above all of them.

BOHR. Otto Hahn - he's still there. He discovered fission, after all.

MARGRETHE. Hahn's a chemist. I thought that what Hahn discovered ...

BOHR. ... was that Enrico Fermi had discovered it in Rome four years earlier. Yes - he just didn't realize it was fission. It didn't occur to anyone that the uranium atom might have split, and turned into an atom of barium and an atom of krypton. Not until Hahn and Strassmann did the analysis, and detected the barium.

MARGRETHE. Fermi's in Chicago.

BOHR. His wife's Jewish.

MARGRETHE. So Heisenberg would be in charge of the work?

BOHR. Margrethe, there is no work! John Wheeler and I did it all in 1939. One of the implications of our paper is that there's no way in the foreseeable future in which fission can be used to produce any kind of weapon.

MARGRETHE. Then why is everyone still working on it?

BOHR. Because there's an element of magic in it. You fire a neutron at the nucleus of a uranium atom and it splits into two other elements. It's what the alchemists were trying to do - to turn one element into another.

MARGRETHE. So why is he coming?

BOHR. Now your curiosity's aroused.

MARGRETHE. My forebodings.

HEISENBERG. I crunch over the familiar gravel to the Bohrs' front door, and tug at the familiar bell-pull. Fear, yes. And another sensation, that's become painfully familiar over the past year. A mixture of self-importance and sheer helpless absurdity - that of all the 2,000 million people in this world, I'm the one who's been charged with this impossible responsibility.... The heavy door swings open.

BOHR. My dear Heisenberg!

HEISENBERG. My dear Bohr!

BOHR Come in, come in....

MARGRETHE. And of course as soon as they catch sight of each other all their caution disappears. The old flames leap up from the ashes. If we can just negotiate all the treacherous little opening civilities ...

HEISENBERG. I'm so touched you felt able to ask me.

BOHR. We must try to go on behaving like human beings.

HEISENBERG. I realize how awkward it is.

BOHR. We scarcely had a chance to do more than shake hands at lunch the other day.

HEISENBERG. And Margrethe I haven't seen ...

BOHR. Since you were here four years ago.

MARGRETHE. Niels is right. You look older.

HEISENBERG. I had been hoping to see you both in 1938, at the congress in Warsaw ...

BOHR. I believe you had some personal trouble.

HEISENBERG. A little business in Berlin.

MARGRETHE. In the Prinz-Albrecht-Strasse?

HEISENBERG. A slight misunderstanding.

BOHR. We heard, yes. I'm so sorry.

HEISENBERG. These things happen. The question is now resolved. Happily resolved. We should all have met in Zürich ...

BOHR. In September 1939.

HEISENBERG. Only of course ...

MARGRETHE. There was an unfortunate clash with the outbreak of war.

HEISENBERG. Sadly.

BOHR. Sadly for us, certainly.

MARGRETHE. A lot more sadly still for many people.

HEISENBERG. Yes. Indeed.

BOHR. Well, there it is.

HEISENBERG. What can I say?

MARGRETHE. What can any of us say, in the present circumstances?

HEISENBERG. No. And your sons?

MARGRETHE. Are well, thank you. Elisabeth? The children?

HEISENBERG. Very well. They send their love, of course.

MARGRETHE. They so much wanted to see each other, in spite

of everything! But now the moment has come they're so busy avoiding each other's eye that they can scarcely see each other at all.

HEISENBERG. I wonder if you realize how much it means to me to be back here in Copenhagen. In this house. I have become rather isolated in these last few years.

BOHR. I can imagine.

MARGRETHE. Me he scarcely notices. I watch him discreetly from behind my expression of polite interest as he struggles on.

HEISENBERG. Have things here been difficult?

BOHR. Difficult?

MARGRETHE. Of course. He has to ask. He has to get it out of the way.

BOHR. Difficult.... What can I say? We've not so far been treated to the gross abuses that have occurred elsewhere. The race laws have not been enforced.

MARGRETHE. Yet.

BOHR. A few months ago they started deporting Communists and other anti-German elements.

HEISENBERG. But you personally ...?

BOHR. Have been left strictly alone.

HEISENBERG. I've been anxious about you.

BOHR. Kind of you. No call for sleepless nights in Leipzig so far, though.

MARGRETHE. Another silence. He's done his duty. Now he can begin to steer the conversation round to pleasanter subjects.

HEISENBERG. Are you still sailing?

BOHR. Sailing?

MARGRETHE. Not a good start.

BOHR. No, no sailing.

HEISENBERG. The Sound is ...?

BOHR. Mined.

HEISENBERG. Of course.

MARGRETHE. I assume he won't ask if Niels has been skiing.

HEISENBERG. You've managed to get some skiing?

BOHR. Skiing? In Denmark?

HEISENBERG. In Norway. You used to go to Norway.

BOHR. I did, yes.

HEISENBERG. But since Norway is also ... well ...

BOHR. Also occupied? Yes, that might make it easier. In fact I suppose we could now holiday almost anywhere in Europe.

HEISENBERG. I'm sorry. I hadn't thought of it quite in those terms.

BOHR. Perhaps I'm being a little oversensitive.

HEISENBERG. Of course not. I should have thought.

MARGRETHE. He must almost be starting to wish he was back in the Prinz-Albrecht-Strasse.

HEISENBERG. I don't suppose you feel you could ever come to Germany ...

MARGRETHE. The boy's an idiot.

BOHR. My dear Heisenberg, it would be an easy mistake to make, to think that the citizens of a small nation, of a small nation overrun, wantonly and cruelly overrun, by its more powerful neighbor, don't have exactly the same feelings of national pride as their conquerors, exactly the same love of their country.

MARGRETHE. Niels, we agreed.

BOHR. To talk about physics, yes.

MARGRETHE. Not about politics.

BOHR. I'm sorry.

HEISENBERG. No, no - I was simply going to say that I still have my old ski hut at Bayrischzell. So if by any chance ... at any time ... for any reason ...

BOHR. Perhaps Margrethe would be kind enough to sew a yellow star on my ski jacket.

HEISENBERG Yes. Yes. Stupid of me.

MARGRETHE. Silence again. Those first brief sparks have disappeared, and the ashes have become very cold indeed. So now of course I'm starting to feel almost sorry for him. Sitting here all on his own in the midst of people who hate him, all on his own against the two of us. He looks younger again, like the boy who first came here in 1924. Younger than Christian would have been now. Shy and arrogant and anxious to be loved. Homesick and pleased to be away from home at last. And, yes, it's sad, because Niels loved him, he was a father to him.

HEISENBERG. So ... what are you working on?

MARGRETHE. And all he can do is press forward.

BOHR. Fission, mostly.

HEISENBERG. I saw a couple of papers in the Physical Review. The velocity-range relations of fission fragments ...?

BOHR. And something about the interactions of nuclei with deuterons. And you?

HEISENBERG. Various things.

MARGRETHE. Fission?

HEISENBERG. I sometimes feel very envious of your cyclotron.

MARGRETHE. Why? Are you working on fission yourself?

HEISENBERG. There are over thirty in the United States. Whereas in the whole of Germany ... Well ... You still get to your country place, at any rate?

BOHR. We still go to Tisvilde, yes.

MARGRETHE. In the whole of Germany, you were going to say ...

BOHR. ... there is not one single cyclotron.

HEISENBERG. So beautiful at this time of year. Tisvilde.

BOHR. You haven't come to borrow the cyclotron, have you? That's not why you've come to Copenhagen?

HEISENBERG. That's not why I've come to Copenhagen.

BOHR. I'm sorry. We mustn't jump to conclusions.

HEISENBERG. No, we must none of us jump to conclusions of any sort.

MARGRETHE. We must wait patiently to be told.

HEISENBERG. It's not always easy to explain things to the world at large.

BOHR. I realize that we must always be conscious of the wider audience our words may have. But the lack of cyclotrons in Germany is surely not a military secret.

HEISENBERG. I've no idea what's a secret and what isn't.

BOHR. No secret, either, about why there aren't any. You can't say it but I can. It's because the Nazis have systematically undermined theoretical physics. Why? Because so many people working in the field were Jews. And why were so many of them Jews? Because theoretical physics, the sort of physics done by Einstein, by Schrödinger and Pauli, by Born and Sommerfold, by you and me, was always regarded in Germany as inferior to experimental physics, and the theoretical chairs and lectureships were the only ones that Jews could get.

MARGRETHE. Physics, yes? Physics.

BOHR. This is physics.

MARGRETHE. It's also politics.

HEISENBERG. The two are sometimes painfully difficult to keep apart.

BOHR. So, you saw those two papers. I haven't seen anything by you recently.

HEISENBERG. No.

BOHR. Not like you. Too much teaching?

HEISENBERG. I'm not teaching. Not at the moment.

BOHR. My dear Heisenberg - they haven't pushed you out of your chair at Leipzig? That's not what you've come to tell us?

HEISENBERG. No, I'm still at Leipzig. For part of each week.

BOHR. And for the rest of the week?

HEISENBERG. Elsewhere. The problem is more work, not less.

BOHR. I see. Do I?

HEISENBERG. Are you in touch with any of our friends in England? Born? Chadwick?

BOHR. Heisenberg, we're under German occupation. Germany's at war with Britain.

HEISENBERG. I thought you might still have contacts of some sort. Or people in America? We're not at war with America.

MARGRETHE. Yet.

HEISENBERG. You've heard nothing from Pauli, in Princeton? Goudsmit? Fermi?

BOHR. What do you want to know?

HEISENBERG. I was simply curious.... I was thinking about Robert Oppenheimer the other day. I had a great set-to with him in Chicago in 1939.

BOHR. About mesons.

HEISENBERG. Is he still working on mesons?

BOHR. I'm quite out of touch.

MARGRETHE. The only foreign visitor we've had was from Germany. Your friend Weizsäcker was here in March.

HEISENBERG. *My* friend? *Your* friend, too. I hope. You know he's come back to Copenhagen with me? He's very much hoping to see you again.

MARGRETHE. When he came here in March he brought the head of the German Cultural Institute with him.

HEISENBERG. I'm sorry about that. He did it with the best of intentions. He may not have explained to you that the Institute is run by the Cultural Division of the Foreign Office. We have good friends in the foreign service. Particularly at the Embassy here.

BOHR. Of course. I knew his father when he was Ambassador in Copenhagen in the twenties.

HEISENBERG. It hasn't changed so much since then, you know, the German foreign service.

BOHR. It's a department of the Nazi government..

HEISENBERG. Germany is more complex than it may perhaps appear from the outside. The different organs of state have quite different traditions, in spite of all attempts at reform. Particularly the foreign service. Our people in the Embassy here are quite old-fashioned in the way they use their influence. They would certainly be trying to see that distinguished local citizens were able to work undisturbed.

BOHR. Are you telling me that I'm being protected by your friends in the Embassy?

HEISENBERG. What I'm saying, in case Weizsäcker failed to make it clear, is that you would find congenial company there. I know people would be very honored if you felt able to accept an occasional invitation.

BOHR. To cocktail parties at the Germany Embassy? To coffee and cakes with the Nazi plenipotentiary?

HEISENBERG. To lectures, perhaps. To discussion groups. Social contacts of any sort could be helpful.

BOHR. I'm sure they could.

HEISENBERG. Essential, perhaps, in certain circumstances.

BOHR. In what circumstances?

HEISENBERG. I think we both know.

BOHR. Because I'm half Jewish?

HEISENBERG. We all at one time or another may need the help of our friends.

BOHR. Is this why you've come to Copenhagen? To invite me to watch the deportation of my fellow-Danes from a grandstand seat in the windows of the German Embassy?

HEISENBERG. Bohr, please! Please! What else can I do? How else can I help? It's an impossibly difficult situation for you, I understand that. It's also an impossibly difficult one for me.

BOHR. Yes. I'm sorry. I'm sure you also have the best of intentions.

HEISENBERG. Forget what I said. Unless ...

BOHR. Unless I need to remember it.

HEISENBERG. In any case it's not why I've come.

MARGRETHE. Perhaps you should simply say what it is you want to say.

HEISENBERG. What you and I often used to do in the old days was to take an evening stroll.

BOHR. Often. Yes. In the old days.

HEISENBERG. You don't feel like a stroll this evening, for old times' sake?

BOHR. A little chilly tonight, perhaps, for strolling.

HEISENBERG. This is so difficult. You remember where we first met?

BOHR. Of course. At Göttingen in 1922.

HEISENBERG. At a lecture festival held in your honor.

BOHR. It was a high honor. I was very conscious of it.

HEISENBERG. You were being honored for two reasons. Firstly because you were a great physicist ...

BOHR. Yes, yes.

HEISENBERG. ... and secondly because you were one of the very few people in Europe who were prepared to have dealings with Germany. The war had been over for four years, and we were still lepers. You held out your hand to us. You've always inspired love, you know that. Wherever you've been, wherever you've worked. Here in Denmark. In England, in America. But in Germany we worshipped you. Because you held out your hand to us.

BOHR. Germany's changed.

HEISENBERG. Yes. Then we were down. And you could be generous.

MARGRETHE. And now you're up.

HEISENBERG. And generosity's harder. But you held out your hand to us then, and we took it.

BOHR. Yes.... No! Not you. As a matter of fact. You bit it.

HEISENBERG. Bit it?

BOHR. Bit my hand! You did! I held it out, in my most statesmanlike and reconciliatory way, and you gave it a very nasty nip.

HEISENBERG. *I* did?

BOHR. The first time I ever set eyes on you. At one of those lectures I was giving in Göttingen.

HEISENBERG. What are you talking about?

BOHR. You stood up and laid into me.

HEISENBERG. Oh ... I offered a few comments.

BOHR. Beautiful summer's day. The scent of roses drifting in from the gardens. Rows of eminent physicists and mathematicians, all nodding approval of my benevolence and wisdom. Suddenly up jumps a cheeky young pup and tells me that my mathematics are wrong.

HEISENBERG. They were wrong.

BOHR. How old were you?

HEISENBERG. Twenty.

BOHR. Two years younger than the century.

HEISENBERG. Not quite.

BOHR. December 5th, yes?

HEISENBERG. 1.93 years younger than the century.

BOHR. To be precise.

HEISENBERG. No - to two places of decimals. To be *precise*, 1.928...7...6...7...1...

BOHR. I can always keep track of you, all the same. And the century.

MARGRETHE. And Niels has suddenly decided to love him again, in spite of everything. Why? What happened? Was it the recollection of that summer's day in Göttingen? Or everything? Or nothing at all? Whatever it was, by the time we've sat down to dinner the cold ashes have started into flame once again.

BOHR. You were always so combative! It was the same when we played table tennis at Tisvilde. You looked as if you were trying to kill me.

HEISENBERG. I wanted to win. Of course I wanted to win. *You* wanted to win.

BOHR. I wanted an agreeable game of table tennis.

HEISENBERG. You couldn't see the expression on your face.

BOHR. I could see the expression on yours.

HEISENBERG. What about those games of poker in the ski hut at Bayrischzell, then? You once cleaned us all out! You remember that? With a nonexistent straight! We're all mathematicians - we're all counting the cards - we're 90% certain he hasn't got anything. But on he goes, raising us, raising us. This insane confidence. Until our faith in mathematical probability begins to waver, and one by one we all throw in.

BOHR. I thought I *had* a straight! I misread the cards! I bluffed myself!

MARGRETHE. Poor Niels.

HEISENBERG. Poor Niels? He won! He bankrupted us! You were insanely competitive! He got us all playing poker once with imaginary cards!

BOHR. You played chess with Weizsäcker on an imaginary board!

MARGRETHE. Who won?

BOHR. Need you ask? At Bayrischzell we'd ski down from the hut to get provisions, and he'd make even that into some kind of race! You remember? When we were there with Weizsäcker and someone? You got out a stopwatch.

HEISENBERG. It took poor Weizsäcker eighteen minutes.

BOHR. You were down there in ten, of course.

HEISENBERG. Eight.

BOHR. I don't recall how long I took.

HEISENBERG. Forty-five minutes.

BOHR. Thank you.

MARGRETHE. Some rather swift skiing going on here, I think.

HEISENBERG. Your skiing was like your science. What were you waiting for? Me and Weizsäcker to come back and suggest some slight change of emphasis?

BOHR. Probably.

HEISENBERG. You were doing seventeen drafts of each slalom?

MARGRETHE. And without me there to type them out.

BOHR. At least I knew where I was. At the speed you were going you were up against the uncertainty relationship. If you knew where you were when you were down you didn't know how fast you'd got there. If you knew how fast you'd been going you didn't know you were down.

HEISENBERG. I certainly didn't stop to think about it.

BOHR. Not to criticize, but that's what might be criticized with some of your science.

HEISENBERG. I usually got there, all the same.

BOHR. You never cared what got destroyed on the way, though. As long as the mathematics worked out you were satisfied.

HEISENBERG. If something works it works.

BOHR. But the question is always, What does the mathematics mean, in plain language? What are the philosophical implications?

HEISENBERG. I always knew you'd be picking your way step by step down the slope behind me, digging all the capsized meanings and implications out of the snow.

MARGRETHE. The faster you ski the sooner you're across the cracks and crevasses.

HEISENBERG. The faster you ski the better you think.

BOHR. Not to disagree, but that is most ... most interesting.

HEISENBERG. By which you mean it's nonsense. But it's not nonsense. Decisions make themselves when you're coming downhill at seventy kilometers an hour. Suddenly there's the edge of nothingness in front of you. Swerve left? Swerve right? Or think about it and die? In your head you swerve both ways ...

MARGRETHE. Like that particle.

HEISENBERG. What particle?

MARGRETHE. The one that you said goes through two different slits at the same time.

HEISENBERG. Oh, in our old thought-experiment. Yes. Yes!

MARGRETHE. Or Schrödinger's wretched cat.

HEISENBERG. That's alive and dead at the same time.

MARGRETHE. Poor beast.

BOHR. My love, it was an imaginary cat.

MARGRETHE. I know.

BOHR. Locked away with an imaginary phial of cyanide.

MARGRETHE. I know, I know.

HEISENBERG. So the particle's here, the particle's there ...

BOHR. The cat's alive, the cat's dead ...

MARGRETHE. You've swerved left, you've swerved right ...

HEISENBERG. Until the experiment is over, this is the point, until the sealed chamber is opened, the abyss detoured; and it turns out that the particle has met itself again, the cat's dead ...

MARGRETHE. And you're alive.

BOHR. Not so fast, Heisenberg ...

HEISENBERG. The swerve itself was the decision.

BOHR. Not so fast, not so fast!

HEISENBERG. Isn't that how you shot Hendrik Casimir dead?

BOHR. Hendrik Casimir?

HEISENBERG. When he was working here at the Institute.

BOHR. I never shot Hendrik Casimir.

HEISENBERG. You told me you did.

BOHR. It was George Gamow. I shot George Gamow. *You* don't know - it was long after your time.

HEISENBERG. Bohr, you shot Hendrik Casimir.

BOHR. Gamow, Gamow. Because he insisted that it was always quicker to act than to react. To make a decision to do something rather than respond to someone else's doing it.

HEISENBERG. And for that you shot him?

BOHR. It was him! He went out and bought a pair of pistols! He puts one in his pocket, I put one in mine, and we get on with the day's work. Hours go by, and we're arguing ferociously about - I can't remember - our problems with the nitrogen nucleus, I expect - when suddenly Gamow reaches into his pocket ...

HEISENBERG. Cap pistols.

BOHR. Cap pistols, yes. Of course.

HEISENBERG. Margrethe was looking a little worried.

MARGRETHE. No - a little surprised. At the turn of events.

BOHR. Now you remember how quick he was.

HEISENBERG. Casimir?

BOHR. Gamow.

HEISENBERG. Not as quick as me.

BOHR. Of course not. But compared with me.

HEISENBERG. A fast neutron. However, or so you're going to tell me ...

BOHR. However, yes, before his gun is even out of his pocket ...

HEISENBERG. You've drafted your reply.

MARGRETHE. I've typed it out.

HEISENBERG. You've checked it with Klein.

MARGRETHE. I've retyped it.

HEISENBERG. You've submitted it to Pauli in Hamburg.

MARGRETHE. I've retyped it again.

BOHR. Before his gun is even out of his pocket, mine is in my hand.

HEISENBERG. And poor Casimir has been blasted out of existence.

BOHR. Except that it was Gamow.

HEISENBERG. It was Casimir! He told me!

BOHR. Yes, well, one of the two.

HEISENBERG. Both of them simultaneously alive and dead in our memories.

BOHR. Like a pair of Schrödinger cats. Where were we?

HEISENBERG. Skiing. Or music. That's another thing that decides everything for you. I play the piano and the way seems to open in front of me - all I have to do is follow. That's how I had my one success with women. At a musical evening at the Bückings in Leipzig - we've assembled a piano trio. 1937, just when all my troubles with the... when my troubles are coming to a head. We're playing the Beethoven G major. We finish the scherzo, and I look up from the piano to see if the others are ready to start the final presto. And in that instant I catch a glimpse of a young woman sitting at the side of the room. Just the briefest glimpse, but of course at once I've carried her off to Bayrischzell, we're engaged, we're married, etc - the usual hopeless romantic fantasies. Then off we go into the presto, and it's terrifyingly fast - so fast there's no time to be afraid. And suddenly everything in the world seems easy. We reach the end and I just carry on skiing. Get myself introduced to the young woman - see her home - and, yes, a week later I've carried her off to Bayrischzell - another week and we're engaged - three months and we're married. All on the sheer momentum of that presto!

BOHR. You were saying you felt isolated. But you do have a

companion, after all.

HEISENBERG. Music?

BOHR. Elisabeth!

HEISENBERG. Oh. Yes. Though, what with the children, and so on ... I've always envied the way you and Margrethe manage to talk about everything. Your work. Your problems. Me, no doubt.

BOHR. I was formed by nature to be a mathematically curious entity: not one but half of two.

HEISENBERG. Mathematics becomes very odd when you apply it to people. One plus one can add up to so many different sums ...

MARGRETHE. Silence. What's he thinking about now? His life? Or ours?

BOHR. So many things we think about at the same time. Our lives and our physics.

MARGRETHE. All the things that come into our heads out of nowhere.

BOHR. Our private consolations. Our private agonies.

HEISENBERG. Silence. And of course they're thinking about their children again.

MARGRETHE. The same bright things. The same dark things. Back and back they come.

HEISENBERG. Their four children living, and their two children dead.

MARGRETHE. Harald. Lying alone in that ward.

BOHR. She's thinking about Christian and Harald.

HEISENBERG. The two lost boys. Harald ...

BOHR. All those years alone in that terrible ward.

HEISENBERG. And Christian. The firstborn. The eldest son.

BOHR. And once again I see those same few moments that I see every day.

HEISENBERG. Those short moments on the boat, when the tiller slams over in the heavy sea, and Christian is falling.

BOHR. If I hadn't let him take the helm ...

HEISENBERG. Those long moments in the water.

BOHR. Those endless moments in the water.

HEISENBERG. When he's struggling towards the lifebuoy.

BOHR. So near to touching it.

MARGRETHE. I'm at Tisvilde. I look up from my work. There's

Niels in the doorway, silently watching me. He turns his head away, and I know at once what's happened.

BOHR. So near, so near! So slight a thing!

HEISENBERG. Again and again the tiller slams over. Again and again ...

MARGRETHE. Niels turns his head away ...

BOHR. Christian reaches for the lifebuoy ...

HEISENBERG. But about some things even they never speak.

BOHR. About some things even we only think.

MARGRETHE. Because there's nothing to be said.

BOHR. Well ... perhaps we *should* be warm enough. You suggested a stroll.

HEISENBERG. In fact the weather is remarkably warm.

BOHR. We shan't be long.

HEISENBERG. A week at most.

BOHR. What - our great hike through Zealand?

HEISENBERG. We went to Elsinore. I often think about what you said there.

BOHR. You don't mind, my love? Half an hour?

HEISENBERG. An hour, perhaps. No, the whole appearance of Elsinore, you said, was changed by our knowing that Hamlet had lived there. Every dark corner there reminds us of the darkness inside the human soul ...

MARGRETHE. So, they're walking again. He's done it. And if they're walking they're talking. Talking in a rather different way, no doubt - I've typed out so much in my time about how differently particles behave when they're unobserved.... I knew Niels would never hold out if they could just get through the first few minutes. If only out of curiosity.... Now they're started an hour will mean two, of course, perhaps three.... The first thing they ever did was to go for a walk together. At Göttingen, after that lecture. Niels immediately went to look for the presumptuous young man who'd queried his mathematics, and swept him off for a tramp in the country. Walk - talk - make his acquaintance. And when Heisenberg arrived here to work for him, off they go again, on their great tour of Zealand. A lot of this century's physics they did in the open air. Strolling around the forest paths at Tisvilde. Going down to the beach with the children. Heisenberg holding Christian's hand. Yes, and every evening in Copenhagen, after dinner, they'd walk round Faelled Park behind the Institute, or out along Langlinie into the harbor. Walk, and talk. Long, long before walls had ears.... But this time, in 1941, their walk takes a different course. Ten minutes after they set out ... they're back! I've scarcely had the table cleared when there's Niels in the doorway. I see at once how upset he is - he can't look me in the eye.

BOHR. Heisenberg wants to say goodbye. He's leaving.

MARGRETHE. *He* won't look at me, either.

HEISENBERG. Thank you. A delightful evening. Almost like old times. So kind of you.

MARGRETHE. You'll have some coffee? A glass of something?

HEISENBERG. I have to get back and prepare for my lecture.

MARGRETHE. But you'll come and see us again before you leave?

BOHR. He has a great deal to do.

MARGRETHE. It's like the worst moments of 1927 all over again, when Niels came back from Norway and first read Heisenberg's uncertainty paper. Something they both seemed to have forgotten about earlier in the evening, though I hadn't. Perhaps they've both suddenly remembered that time. Only from the look on their faces something even worse has happened.

HEISENBERG. Forgive me if I've done or said anything that ...

BOHR. Yes, yes.

HEISENBERG. It meant a great deal to me, being here with you both again. More perhaps than you realize.

MARGRETHE. It was a pleasure for us. Our love to Elisabeth.

BOHR. Of course.

MARGRETHE. And the children.

HEISENBERG. Perhaps, when this war is over.... If we're all spared.... Goodbye.

MARGRETHE. Politics?

BOHR. Physics. He's not right, though. How can he be right? John Wheeler and I ...

MARGRETHE. A breath of air as we talk, why not?

BOHR. A breath of air?

MARGRETHE. A turn around the garden. Healthier than staying indoors, perhaps.

BOHR. Oh. Yes.

MARGRETHE. For everyone concerned.

BOHR. Yes. Thank you ... How can he possibly be right? Wheeler and I went through the whole thing in 1939.

MARGRETHE. What did he say?

BOHR. Nothing. I don't know. I was too angry to take it in.

MARGRETHE. Something about fission?

BOHR. What happens in fission? You fire a neutron at a uranium nucleus, it splits, and it releases energy.

MARGRETHE. A huge amount of energy. Yes?

BOHR. About enough to move a speck of dust. But it also releases two or three more neutrons. Each of which has the chance of splitting another nucleus.

MARGRETHE. So then those two or three split nuclei each release energy in their turn?

BOHR. And two or three more neutrons.

HEISENBERG. You start a trickle of snow sliding as you ski. The trickle becomes a snowball ...

BOHR. An ever-widening chain of split nuclei forks through the uranium, doubling and quadrupling in millionths of a second from one generation to the next. First two splits, let's say for simplicity. Then two squared, two cubed, two to the fourth, two to the fifth, two to the sixth ...

HEISENBERG. The thunder of the gathering avalanche echoes from all the surrounding mountains ...

BOHR. Until eventually, after let's say eighty generations, 2^{80} specks of dust have been moved. 2^{80} is a number with 24 noughts. Enough specks of dust to constitute a city, and all who live in it.

HEISENBERG. But there is a catch.

BOHR. There is a catch, thank God. Natural uranium consists of two different isotopes, U-238 and U-235. Most of it's U-238, which you can only fission with fast neutrons. Most neutrons, though, will only fission the other isotope, U-235 - and less than one percent of natural uranium is U-235.

HEISENBERG. This was Bohr's great insight. Another of his

amazing intuitions. It came to him when he was at Princeton in 1939, walking across the campus with Wheeler. A characteristic Bohr moment - I wish I'd been there to enjoy it. Five minutes deep silence as they walked, then: 'Now hear this - I have understood everything.'

BOHR. In fact it's a double catch, because the 238 also slows neutrons down and absorbs them. So an explosive chain reaction will never occur in natural uranium. To make an explosion you will have to separate out pure 235. And to make the chain long enough for a large explosion ...

HEISENBERG. Eighty generations, let's say ...

BOHR. ... you would need many tons of it. And it's extremely difficult to separate.

HEISENBERG. Tantalizingly difficult.

BOHR. Mercifully difficult. The best estimates, when I was in America in 1939, were that to produce even one gram of U-235 would take 26,000 years. By which time, surely, this war will be over. So he's wrong, you see, he's wrong! Or could *I* be wrong? Could I have miscalculated? Let me see.... What are the absorption rates for fast neutrons in 238? What's the mean free path of slow neutrons in 235 ...?

MARGRETHE. But what exactly had Heisenberg said? That's what everyone wanted to know, then and forever after.

BOHR. It's what the British wanted to know, as soon as Chadwick managed to get in touch with me. What exactly did Heisenberg say?

HEISENBERG. And what exactly did Bohr reply? That was of course the first thing my colleagues asked me when I got back to Germany.

MARGRETHE. What did Heisenberg tell Niels - what did Niels reply? The person who wanted to know most of all was Heisenberg himself.

BOHR. You mean when he came back to Copenhagen after the war, in 1947?

MARGRETHE. Escorted this time not by unseen agents of the Gestapo, but by a very conspicuous minder from British intelligence.

BOHR. I think he wanted various things.

MARGRETHE. Two things. Food-parcels ...

BOHR. For his family in Germany. They were on the verge of starvation.

MARGRETHE. And for you to agree what you'd said to each other in 1941.

BOHR. The conversation went wrong almost as fast as it did before.

MARGRETHE. You couldn't even agree where you'd walked that night.

HEISENBERG. Where we walked? Faelled Park, of course. Where we went so often in the old days.

MARGRETHE. But Faelled Park is behind the Institute, four kilometers away from where we live!

HEISENBERG. I can see the drift of autumn leaves under the street lamps next to the bandstand.

BOHR. Yes, because you remember it as October!

MARGRETHE. And it was September.

BOHR. No fallen leaves!

MARGRETHE. And it was 1941. No street lamps!

BOHR. I thought we hadn't got any further than my study. What I can see is the drift of papers under the reading lamp on my desk.

HEISENBERG. We must have been outside! What I was going to say was treasonable. If I'd been overheard I'd have been executed.

MARGRETHE. So what was this mysterious thing you said?

HEISENBERG. There's no mystery about it. There never was any mystery. I remember it absolutely clearly, because my life was at stake, and I chose my words very carefully. I simply asked you if as a physicist one had the moral right to work on the practical exploitation of atomic energy. Yes?

BOHR. I don't recall.

HEISENBERG. You don't recall, no, because you immediately became alarmed. You stopped dead in your tracks.

BOHR. I was horrified.

HEISENBERG. Horrified. Good, you remember that. You stood there gazing at me, horrified.

BOHR. Because the implication was obvious. That you *were* working on it.

HEISENBERG. And you jumped to the conclusion that I was trying to provide Hitler with nuclear weapons.

BOHR. And you were!

HEISENBERG. No! A reactor! That's what we were trying to build! A machine to produce power! To generate electricity, to drive ships!

BOHR. You didn't say anything about a reactor.

HEISENBERG. I didn't say anything about anything! Not in so many words. I couldn't! I'd no idea how much could be overheard. How much you'd repeat to others.

BOHR. But then I asked you if you actually thought that uranium fission could be used for the construction of weapons.

HEISENBERG. Ah! It's coming back!

BOHR. And I clearly remember what you replied.

HEISENBERG. I said I now knew that it could be.

BOHR. This is what really horrified me.

HEISENBERG. Because you'd always been confident that weapons would need 235, and that we could never separate enough of it.

BOHR. A reactor - yes, maybe, because you can keep a slow chain reaction going in natural uranium.

HEISENBERG. What we'd realized, though, was that if we could once get the reactor going ...

BOHR. The 238 in the natural uranium would absorb the fast neutrons ...

HEISENBERG. Exactly as you predicted in 1939 - everything we were doing was based on that fundamental insight of yours. The 238 would absorb the fast neutrons. And would be transformed by them into a new element altogether.

BOHR. Neptunium. Which would decay in its turn into another new element ...

HEISENBERG. At least as fissile as the 235 that we couldn't separate ...

MARGRETHE. Plutonium.

HEISENBERG. Plutonium.

BOHR. I should have worked it out for myself.

HEISENBERG. If we could build a reactor we could build bombs. That's what had brought me to Copenhagen. But none of this could I say. And at this point you stopped listening. The bomb had already gone off inside your head. I realized we were heading back towards the house. Our walk was over. Our one chance to talk had gone forever.

BOHR. Because I'd grasped the central point already. That one way or another you saw the possibility of supplying Hitler with nuclear weapons.

HEISENBERG. You grasped at least four different central points, all of them wrong. You told Rozental that I'd tried to pick your brains about fission. You told Weisskopf that I'd asked you what you knew about the Allied nuclear program. Chadwick thought I was hoping to persuade you that there was no German program. But then you seem to have told some people that I'd tried to recruit you to work on it!

BOHR. Very well. Let's start all over again from the beginning. No Gestapo in the shadows this time. No British intelligence officer. No one watching us at all.

MARGRETHE. Only me.

BOHR. Only Margrethe. We're going to make the whole thing clear to Margrethe. You know how strongly I believe that we don't do science for ourselves, that we do it so we can explain to others ...

HEISENBERG. In plain language.

BOHR. In plain language. Not your view, I know - you'd be happy to describe what you were up to purely in differential equations if you could - but for Margrethe's sake ...

HEISENBERG. Plain language.

BOHR. Plain language. All right, so here we are, walking along the street once more. And this time I'm absolutely calm, I'm listening intently. What is it you want to say?

HEISENBERG. It's not just what *I* want to say! The whole German nuclear team in Berlin! Not Diebner, of course, not the Nazis - but Weizsäcker, Hahn, Wirtz, Jensen, Houtermanns - they all wanted me to come and discuss it with you. We all see you as a kind of spiritual father.

MARGRETHE. The Pope. That's what you used to call Niels behind his back. And now you want him to give you absolution.
HEISENBERG. Absolution? No!
MARGRETHE. According to your colleague Jensen.
HEISENBERG. Absolution is the last thing I want!
MARGRETHE. You told one historian that Jensen had expressed it perfectly.
HEISENBERG. Did I? Absolution ... Is that what I've come for? It's like trying to remember who was at that lunch you gave me at the Institute. Around the table sit all the different explanations for every-thing I did. I turn to look ... Petersen, Rozental, and ... yes... now the word absolution is taking its place among them all ...
MARGRETHE. Though I thought absolution was granted for sins past and repented, not for sins intended and yet to be committed.
HEISENBERG. Exactly! That's why I was so shocked!
BOHR. *You* were shocked?
HEISENBERG. Because you *did* give me absolution! That's ex-actly what you did! As we were hurrying back to the house. You mut-tered something about everyone in wartime being obliged to do his best for his own country. Yes?
BOHR. Heaven knows what I said. But now here I am, pro-foundly calm and conscious, weighing my words. You don't want ab-solution. I understand. You want me to tell you *not* to do it? All right. I put my hand on your arm. I look you in the eye in my most papal way. Go back to Germany, Heisenberg. Gather your colleagues to-gether in the laboratory. Get up on a table and tell them: 'Niels Bohr says that in his considered judgment supplying a homicidal maniac with an improved instrument of mass murder is ...' What shall I say? '... an interesting idea.' No, not even an interesting idea. '... a really rather seriously uninteresting idea.' What happens? You all fling down your Geiger counters?
HEISENBERG. Obviously not.
BOHR. Because they'll arrest you.
HEISENBERG. Whether they arrest us or not it won't make any difference. In fact it will make things worse. I'm running my program for the Kaiser Wilhelm Institute. But there's a rival one at Army Ord-nance, run by Kurt Diebner, and he's a party member. If I go they'll

simply get Diebner to take over my programme as well. He should be running it anyway. Wirtz and the rest of them only smuggled me in to keep Diebner and the Nazis out of it. My one hope is to remain in control.

BOHR. So you don't want me to say yes and you don't want me to say no.

HEISENBERG. What I want is for you to listen carefully to what I'm going on to say next, instead of running off down the street like a madman.

BOHR. Very well. Here I am, walking very slowly and popishly. And I listen most carefully as you tell me ...

HEISENBERG. That nuclear weapons will require an enormous technical effort.

BOHR. True.

HEISENBERG. That they will suck up huge resources.

BOHR. Huge resources. Certainly.

HEISENBERG. That sooner or later governments will have to turn to scientists and ask whether it's worth committing those resources - whether there's any hope of producing the weapons in time for them to be used.

BOHR. Of course, but ...

HEISENBERG. Wait. So they will have to come to you and me. We are the ones who will have to advise them whether to go ahead or not. In the end the decision will be in our hands, whether we like it or not.

BOHR. And that's what you want to tell me?

HEISENBERG. That's what I want to tell you.

BOHR. That's why you have come all this way, with so much difficulty? That's why you have thrown away nearly twenty years of friendship? Simply to tell me that?

HEISENBERG. Simply to tell you that.

BOHR. But, Heisenberg, this is more mysterious than ever! What are you telling it me *for*? What am I supposed to do about it? The government of occupied Denmark isn't going to come to me and ask me whether we should produce nuclear weapons!

HEISENBERG. No, but sooner or later, if I manage to remain in control of our program, the German government is going to come to *me*! They will ask *me* whether to continue or not! *I* will have to decide what to tell them!

BOHR. Then you have an easy way out of your difficulties. You tell them the simple truth that you've just told me. You tell them how difficult it will be. And perhaps they'll be discouraged. Perhaps they'll lose interest.

HEISENBERG. But, Bohr, where will that lead? What will be the consequences if we manage to fail?

BOHR. What can I possibly tell you that you can't tell yourself?

HEISENBERG. There was a report in a Stockholm paper that the Americans are working on an atomic bomb.

BOHR. Ah. Now it comes, now it comes. Now I understand everything. You think I have contacts with the Americans?

HEISENBERG. You may. It's just conceivable. If anyone in Occupied Europe does it will be you.

BOHR. So you *do* want to know about the Allied nuclear programme.

HEISENBERG. I simply want to know if there is one. Some hint. Some clue. I've just betrayed my country and risked my life to warn you of the German program ...

BOHR. And now I'm to return the compliment?

HEISENBERG. Bohr, I have to know! I'm the one who has to decide! If the Allies are building a bomb, what am I choosing for my country? You said it would be easy to imagine that one might have less love for one's country if it's small and defenseless. Yes, and it would be another easy mistake to make, to think that one loved one's country less because it happened to be in the wrong. Germany is where I was born. Germany is where I became what I am. Germany is all the faces of my childhood, all the hands that picked me up when I fell, all the voices that encouraged me and set me on my way, all the hearts that speak to my heart. Germany is my widowed mother and my impossible brother. Germany is my wife. Germany is our children. I have to know what I'm deciding for them! Is it another defeat? Another nightmare like the nightmare I grew up with? Bohr, my childhood in Munich came to an end in anarchy and civil war. Are more children going to starve, as we did? Are they going to have to spend winter nights as I did when I was a schoolboy, crawling on my hands and knees through the enemy lines, creeping out into the country under cover of darkness in the snow to find food for my family? Are they going to sit up all night, as I did at the age of seventeen, guarding some terrified prisoner, talking to him and talking to him through the small hours, because he's going to be executed in the morning?

BOHR. But, my dear Heisenberg, there's nothing I can tell you. I've no idea whether there's an Allied nuclear program.

HEISENBERG. It's just getting under way even as you and I are talking. And maybe I'm choosing something worse even than defeat. Because the bomb they're building is to be used on us. On the evening of Hiroshima Oppenheimer said it was his one regret. That they hadn't produced the bomb in time to use on Germany.

BOHR. He tormented himself afterwards.

HEISENBERG. Afterwards, yes. At least we tormented ourselves a little beforehand. Did a single one of them stop to think, even for one brief moment, about what they were doing? Did Oppenheimer? Did Fermi, or Teller, or Szilard? Did Einstein, when he wrote to Roosevelt in 1939 and urged him to finance research on the bomb? Did you, when you escaped from Copenhagen two years later, and went to Los Alamos?

BOHR. My dear good Heisenberg, we weren't supplying the bomb to Hitler!

HEISENBERG. You weren't dropping it on Hitler, either. You were dropping it on anyone who was in reach. On old men and women in the street, on mothers and their children. And if you'd produced it in time they would have been my fellow countrymen. My wife. My children. That was the intention. Yes?

BOHR. That was the intention.

HEISENBERG. You never had the slightest conception of what happens when bombs are dropped on cities. Even conventional bombs. None of you ever experienced it. Not a single one of you. I walked back from the center of Berlin to the suburbs one night, after one of the big raids. No transport moving, of course. The whole city on fire. Even the puddles in the streets are burning. They're puddles of molten phosphorus. It gets on your shoes like some kind of incandescent dog-muck - I have to keep scraping it off - as if the streets have been fouled by the hounds of hell. It would have made you laugh - my shoes keep bursting into flame. All around me, I suppose, there are people trapped, people in various stages of burning to death. And all I can think is, How will I ever get hold of another pair of shoes in times like these?

BOHR. You know why Allied scientists worked on the bomb.

HEISENBERG. Of course. Fear.

BOHR. The same fear that was consuming you. Because they were afraid that *you* were working on it.

HEISENBERG. But, Bohr, you could have told them!

BOHR. Told them what?

HEISENBERG. What I told you in 1941! That the choice is in our hands! In mine - in Oppenheimer's! That if I can tell them the simple truth when they ask me, the simple discouraging truth, so can he!

BOHR. This is what you want from me? Not to tell you what the Americans are doing but to stop them?

HEISENBERG. To tell them that we can stop it together.

BOHR. I had no contact with the Americans!

HEISENBERG. You did with the British.

BOHR. Only later.

HEISENBERG. The Gestapo intercepted the message you sent them about our meeting.

MARGRETHE. And passed it to you?

HEISENBERG. Why not? They'd begun to trust me. This is what gave me the possibility of remaining in control of events.

BOHR. Not to criticize, Heisenberg, but if this is your plan in coming to Copenhagen, it's ... what can I say? It's most interesting.

HEISENBERG. It's not a plan. It's a hope. Not even a hope. A microscopically fine thread of possibility. A wild improbability. Worth trying, though, Bohr! Worth trying, surely! But already you're too angry to understand what I'm saying.

MARGRETHE. No - why he's angry is because he *is* beginning to understand! The Germans drive out most of their best physicists because they're Jews. America and Britain give them sanctuary. Now it turns out that this might offer the Allies a hope of salvation. And at once you come howling to Niels begging him to persuade them to give it up.

BOHR. Margrethe, my love, perhaps we should try to express ourselves a little more temperately.

MARGRETHE. But the gall of it! The sheer, breathtaking gall of it!

BOHR. Bold skiing, I have to say.

HEISENBERG. But, Bohr, we're not skiing now! We're not playing table tennis! We're not juggling with cap pistols and non-existent cards! I refused to believe it, when I first heard the news of Hiroshima. I thought that it was just one of the strange dreams we were living in at the time. They'd got stranger and stranger, God knows, as Germany fell into ruins in those last months of the war. But by then we were living in the strangest of them all. The ruins had suddenly vanished - just the way things do in dreams - and all at once we're in a stately home in the middle of the English country-side. We've been rounded up by the British - the whole team, everyone who worked on atomic research - and we've been spirited away. To Farm Hall, in Huntingdonshire, in the water-meadows of the River Ouse. Our families in Germany are starving, and there are we sitting down each evening to an excellent formal dinner with our charming host, the British officer in charge of us. It's like a pre-war house-party - one of those house-parties in a play, that's cut off from any contact with the outside world, where you know the guests have all been invited for some secret sinister purpose. No one knows we're there - no one in England, no one in Germany, not even our families. But the war's over. What's happening? Perhaps, as in a play, we're going to be quietly murdered, one by one. In the mean-while it's all delightfully civilized. I entertain the party with Beethoven piano sonatas. Major Rittner, our hospitable gaoler, reads Dickens to us, to improve our English.... Did these things really happen to me ...? We wait for the point of it all to be revealed to us. Then one evening it is. And it's even more grotesque than the one we were fearing. It's on the radio: you have actually done the deed that we were tormenting ourselves about. That's why we're there, dining with our gracious host, listening to our Dickens. We've been kept locked up to stop us discussing the subject with anyone until it's too late. When Major Rittner tells us I simply refuse to believe it until I hear it with my own ears on the nine o'clock news. We'd no idea how far ahead you'd got. I can't describe the effect it has on us. You play happily with your toy cap pistol. Then someone else picks it up and pulls the trigger... and all at once there's blood everywhere and people screaming, because it wasn't a toy at all ... We sit up half the night, talking about it, trying to take it in. We're all literally in shock.

MARGRETHE. Because it had been done? Or because it wasn't you who'd done it?

HEISENBERG. Both. Both. Otto Hahn wants to kill himself, because it was he who discovered fission, and he can see the blood on his hands. Gerlach, our old government administrator, also wants to die, because his hands are so shamefully clean. You've done it, though. You've built the bomb.

BOHR. Yes.

HEISENBERG. And you've used it on a living target.

BOHR. On a living target.

MARGRETHE. You're not suggesting that Niels did anything wrong in working at Los Alamos?

HEISENBERG. Of course not. Bohr has never done anything wrong.

MARGRETHE. The decision had been taken long before Niels arrived. The bomb would have been built whether Niels had gone or not.

BOHR. In any case, my part was very small.

HEISENBERG. Oppenheimer described you as the team's father-confessor.

BOHR. It seems to be my role in life.

HEISENBERG. He said you made a great contribution.

BOHR. Spiritual, possibly. Not practical.

HEISENBERG. Fermi says it was you who worked out how to trigger the Nagasaki bomb.

BOHR. I put forward an idea.

MARGRETHE. You're not implying that there's anything that *Niels* needs to explain or defend?

HEISENBERG. No one has ever expected him to explain or defend anything. He's a profoundly good man.

BOHR. It's not a question of goodness. I was spared the decision.
HEISENBERG. Yes, and I was not. So explaining and defending myself was how I spent the last thirty years of my life. When I went to America in 1949 a lot of physicists wouldn't even shake my hand. Hands that had actually built the bomb wouldn't touch mine.
MARGRETHE. And let me tell you, if you think you're making it any clearer to me now, you're not.
BOHR. Margrethe, I understand his feelings ...
MARGRETHE. I don't. I'm as angry as you were before! It's so easy to make you feel conscience-stricken. Why should he transfer his burden to you? Because what does he do after his great consultation with you? He goes back to Berlin and tells the Nazis that he can produce atomic bombs!
HEISENBERG. But what I stress is the difficulty of separating 235.
MARGRETHE. You tell them about plutonium.
HEISENBERG. I tell some of the minor officials. I have to keep people's hopes alive!
MARGRETHE. Otherwise they'll send for the other one.
HEISENBERG. Diebner. Very possibly.
MARGRETHE. There's always a Diebner at hand ready to take over our crimes.
HEISENBERG. Diebner might manage to get a little further than me.
BOHR. Diebner?
HEISENBERG. Might. Just possibly might.
BOHR. He hasn't a quarter of your ability!
HEISENBERG. Not a tenth of it. But he has ten times the eagerness to do it. It might be a very different story if it's Diebner who puts the case at our meeting with Albert Speer, instead of me.
MARGRETHE. The famous meeting with Speer.
HEISENBERG. But this is when it counts. This is the real moment of decision. It's June 1942. Nine months after my trip to Copenhagen. All research cancelled by Hitler unless it produces immediate results - and Speer is the sole arbiter of what will qualify. Now, we've just got the first sign that our reactor's going to work. Our first increase in neutrons. Not much - 13% - but it's a start.

BOHR. June 1942? You're slightly ahead of Fermi in Chicago.

HEISENBERG. Only we don't know that. But the RAF have begun terror bombing. They've obliterated half of Lübeck, and the whole center of Rostock and Cologne. We're desperate for new weapons to strike back with. If ever there's a moment to make our case, this is it.

MARGRETHE. You don't ask him for the funding to continue?

HEISENBERG. To continue with the reactor? Of course I do. But I ask for so little that he doesn't take the program seriously.

MARGRETHE. Do you tell him the reactor will produce plutonium?

HEISENBERG. I don't tell him the reactor will produce plutonium. Not Speer, no. I don't tell him the reactor will produce plutonium.

BOHR. A striking omission, I have to admit.

HEISENBERG. And what happens? It works! He gives us barely enough money to keep the reactor program ticking over. And that is the end of the German atomic bomb. That is the end of it.

MARGRETHE. You go on with the reactor, though.

HEISENBERG. We go on with the reactor. Of course. Because now there's no risk of getting it running in time to produce enough plutonium for a bomb. No, we go on with the reactor all right. We work like madmen on the reactor. We have to drag it all the way across Germany, from east to west, from Berlin to Swabia, to get it away from the bombing, to keep it out of the hands of the Russians. Diebner tries to hijack it on the way. We get it away from him, and we set it up in a little village in the Swabian Jura.

BOHR. This is Haigerloch?

HEISENBERG. There's a natural shelter there – the village inn has a wine-cellar cut into the base of a cliff. We dig a hole in the floor for the reactor, and I keep that program going, I keep it under my control, until the bitter end.

BOHR. But, Heisenberg, with respect now, with the greatest respect, you couldn't even keep the reactor under your control. That reactor was going to kill you.

HEISENBERG. It wasn't put to the test. It never went critical.

BOHR. Thank God. Hambro and Perrin examined it after the Allied troops took over. They said it had no cadmium control rods. There was nothing to absorb any excess of neutrons, to slow the reaction down when it overheated.

HEISENBERG. No rods, no.

BOHR. You believed the reaction would be self-limiting.

HEISENBERG. That's what I originally believed.

BOHR. Heisenberg, the reaction would not have been self-limiting.

HEISENBERG. By 1945 I understood that.

BOHR. So if you ever had got it to go critical, it would have melted down, and vanished into the center of the earth!

HEISENBERG. Not at all. We had a lump of cadmium to hand.

BOHR. A *lump* of cadmium? What were you proposing to do with a *lump* of cadmium?

HEISENBERG. Throw it into the water.

BOHR. What water?

HEISENBERG. The heavy water. The moderator that the uranium was immersed in.

BOHR. My dear good Heisenberg, not to criticize, but you'd all gone mad!

HEISENBERG. We were almost there! We had this fantastic neutron growth! We had 670% growth!

BOHR. You'd lost all contact with reality down in that hole!

HEISENBERG. Another week. Another fortnight. That's all we needed!

BOHR. It was only the arrival of the Allies that saved you!

HEISENBERG. We'd almost reached the critical mass! A tiny bit bigger and the chain would sustain itself indefinitely. All we need is a little more uranium. I set off with Weizsäcker to try and get our hands on Diebner's. Another hair-raising journey all the way back across Germany. Constant air raids - no trains - we try bicycles - we never make it! We end up stuck in a little inn somewhere in the middle of nowhere, listening to the thump of bombs falling all round us. And on the radio someone playing the Beethoven G minor cello sonata.

BOHR. And everything was still under your control?

HEISENBERG. Under my control - yes! That's the point! Under my control!

BOHR. Nothing was under anyone's control by that time!

HEISENBERG. Yes, because at last we were free of all constraints! The nearer the end came the faster we could work!

BOHR. You were no longer running that program, Heisenberg. The program was running you.

HEISENBERG. Two more weeks, two more blocks of uranium, and it would have been German physics that achieved the world's first self-sustaining chain reaction.

BOHR. Except that Fermi had already done it in Chicago, two years earlier.

HEISENBERG. We didn't know that.

BOHR. You didn't know anything down in that cave. You were as blind as moles in a hole. Perrin said that there wasn't even anything to protect you all from the radiation.

HEISENBERG. We didn't have time to think about it.

BOHR. So if it *had* gone critical ...

MARGRETHE. You'd all have died of radiation sickness.

BOHR. My dear Heisenberg! My dear boy!

HEISENBERG. Yes, but by then the reactor would have been running.

BOHR. I should have been there to look after you.

HEISENBERG. That's all we could think of at the time. To get the reactor running, to get the reactor running.

BOHR. You always needed me there to slow you down a little. Your own walking lump of cadmium.

HEISENBERG. If I had died then, what should I have missed? Thirty years of attempting to explain. Thirty years of reproach and hostility. Even you turned your back on me.

MARGRETHE. You came to Copenhagen again. You came to Tisvilde.

HEISENBERG. It was never the same.

BOHR. No. It was never the same.

HEISENBERG. I sometimes think that those final few weeks at Haigerloch were the last happy time in my life. In a strange way it was very peaceful. Suddenly we were out of all the politics of Berlin. Out of the bombing. The war was coming to an end. There was nothing to think about except the reactor. And we didn't go mad, in fact. We didn't work all the time. There was a monastery on top of the rock above our cave. I used to retire to the organ-loft in the church, and play Bach fugues.

MARGRETHE. Look at him. He's lost. He's like a lost child. He's been out in the woods all day, running here, running there. He's shown off, he's been brave, he's been cowardly. He's done wrong, he's done right. And now the evening's come, and all he wants is to go home, and he's lost.

HEISENBERG. Silence.

BOHR. Silence.

MARGRETHE. Silence.

HEISENBERG. And once again the tiller slams over, and Christian is falling.

BOHR. Once again he's struggling towards the lifebuoy.

MARGRETHE. Once again I look up from my work, and there's Niels in the doorway, silently watching me ...

BOHR. So, Heisenberg, why did you come to Copenhagen in 1941? It was right that you told us about all the fears you had. But you didn't really think I'd tell you whether the Americans were working on a bomb.

HEISENBERG. No.

BOHR. You didn't seriously hope that I'd stop them.

HEISENBERG. No.

BOHR. You were going back to work on that reactor whatever I said.

HEISENBERG. Yes.

BOHR. So, Heisenberg, why did you come?

HEISENBERG. Why did I come?

BOHR. Tell us once again. Another draft of the paper. And this time we shall get it right. This time we shall understand.

MARGRETHE. Maybe you'll even understand yourself.

BOHR. After all, the workings of the atom were difficult to explain. We made many attempts. Each time we tried they became more obscure. We got there in the end, however. So - another draft, another draft.

HEISENBERG. Why did I come? And once again I go through that evening in 1941. I crunch over the familiar gravel, and tug at the

familiar bell-pull. What's in my head? Fear, certainly, and the absurd
and horrible importance of someone bearing bad news. But ... yes ...
something else as well. Here it comes again. I can almost see its face.
Something good. Something bright and eager and hopeful.

BOHR. I open the door ...

HEISENBERG. And there he is. I see his eyes light up at the
sight of me.

BOHR. He's smiling his wary schoolboy smile.

HEISENBERG. And I feel a moment of such consolation.

BOHR. A flash of such pure gladness.

HEISENBERG. As if I'd come home after a long journey.

BOHR. As if a long-lost child had appeared on the doorstep.

HEISENBERG. Suddenly I'm free of all the dark tangled currents
in the water.

BOHR. Christian is alive, Harald still unborn.

HEISENBERG. The world is at peace again.

MARGRETHE. Look at them. Father and son still. Just for a moment. Even now we're all dead.

BOHR. For a moment, yes, it's the twenties again.

HEISENBERG. And we shall speak to each other and understand
each other in the way we did before.

MARGRETHE. And from those two heads the future will
emerge. Which cities will be destroyed, and which survive. Who will
die, and who will live. Which world will go down to obliteration, and
which will triumph.

BOHR. My dear Heisenberg!

HEISENBERG. My dear Bohr!

BOHR. Come in, come in ...

ACT TWO

HEISENBERG. It was the very beginning of spring. The first time I came to Copenhagen, in 1924. March: raw, blustery northern weather. But every now and then the sun would come out and leave that first marvelous warmth of the year on your skin. That first breath of returning life.

BOHR. You were twenty-two. So I must have been ...

HEISENBERG. Thirty-eight.

BOHR. Almost the same age as you were when you came in 1941.

HEISENBERG. So what do we do?

BOHR. Put on our boots and rucksacks ...

HEISENBERG. Take the tram to the end of the line ...

BOHR. And start walking!

HEISENBERG. Northwards to Elsinore.

BOHR. If you walk you talk.

HEISENBERG. Then westwards to Tisvilde.

BOHR. And back by way of Hillerød.

HEISENBERG. Walking, talking, for a hundred miles.

BOHR. After which we talked more or less non-stop for the next three years.

HEISENBERG. We'd split a bottle of wine over dinner in your flat at the Institute.

BOHR. Then I'd come up to your room ...

HEISENBERG. That terrible little room in the servants' quarters in the attic.

BOHR. And we'd talk on into the small hours.

HEISENBERG. How, though?

BOHR. How?

HEISENBERG. How did we talk? In Danish?

BOHR. In German, surely.

HEISENBERG. I lectured in Danish. I had to give my first collo-quium when I'd only been here for ten weeks.

BOHR. I remember it. Your Danish was already excellent.

HEISENBERG. No. You did a terrible thing to me. Half an hour before it started you said casually, Oh, I think we'll speak English to-day.

BOHR. But when you explained ...?

HEISENBERG. Explain to the Pope? I didn't dare. That excellent Danish you heard was my first attempt at English.

BOHR. My dear Heisenberg! On our own together, though? My love, do you recall?

MARGRETHE. What language you spoke when I wasn't there? You think I had microphones hidden?

BOHR. No, no - but patience, my love, patience!

MARGRETHE. Patience?

BOHR. You sounded a little sharp.

MARGRETHE. Not at all.

BOHR. We have to follow the threads right back to the beginning of the maze.

MARGRETHE. I'm watching every step.

BOHR. You didn't mind? I hope.

MARGRETHE. Mind?

BOHR. Being left at home?

MARGRETHE. While you went off on your hike? Of course not. Why should I have minded? You had to get out of the house. Two new sons arriving on top of each other would be rather a lot for any man to put up with.

BOHR. Two new sons?

MARGRETHE. Heisenberg.

BOHR. Yes, yes.

MARGRETHE. And our own son.

BOHR. Aage?

MARGRETHE. Ernest!

BOHR. 1924 - of course - Ernest.

MARGRETHE. Number five. Yes?

BOHR. Yes, yes, yes. And if it was March, you're right - he couldn't have been much more than ...

MARGRETHE. One week.

BOHR. One week? One week, yes. And you really didn't mind?

MARGRETHE. Not at all. I was pleased you had an excuse to get away. And you always went off hiking with your new assistants. You went off with Kramers, when he arrived in 1916.

BOHR. Yes, when I suppose Christian was still only ...

MARGRETHE. One week.

BOHR. Yes ... Yes ... I almost killed Kramers, you know.

HEISENBERG. Not with a cap pistol?

BOHR. With a mine. On our walk.

HEISENBERG. Oh, the mine. Yes, you told me, on ours. Never mind Kramers - you almost killed yourself!

BOHR. A mine washed up in the shallows ...

HEISENBERG. And of course at once they compete to throw stones at it. What were you thinking of?

BOHR. I've no idea.

HEISENBERG. A touch of Elsinore there, perhaps.

BOHR. Elsinore?

HEISENBERG. The darkness inside the human soul.

BOHR. You did something just as idiotic.

HEISENBERG. *I* did?

BOHR. With Dirac in Japan. You climbed a pagoda.

HEISENBERG. Oh, the pagoda.

BOHR. Then balanced on the pinnacle. According to Dirac. On one foot. In a high wind. I'm glad I wasn't there.

HEISENBERG. Elsinore, I confess.

BOHR. Elsinore, certainly.

HEISENBERG. I was jealous of Kramers, you know.

BOHR. His Eminence. Isn't that what you called him?

HEISENBERG. Because that's what he was. Your leading cardinal. Your favorite son. Till I arrived on the scene.

MARGRETHE. He was a wonderful cellist.

BOHR. He was a wonderful everything.

HEISENBERG. Far too wonderful.

MARGRETHE. I liked him.

HEISENBERG. I was terrified of him. When I first started at the Institute. I was terrified of all of them. All the boy wonders you had here - they were all so brilliant and accomplished. But Kramers was the heir apparent. All the rest of us had to work in the general study hall. Kramers had the private office next to yours, like the electron on the inmost orbit around the nucleus. And he didn't think much of my physics. He insisted you could explain everything about the atom by classical mechanics.

BOHR. Well, he was wrong.

MARGRETHE. And very soon the private office was vacant.

BOHR. And there was another electron on the inmost orbit.

HEISENBERG. Yes, and for three years we lived inside the atom.

BOHR. With other electrons on the outer orbits around us all over Europe.

HEISENBERG. Max Born and Pascual Jordan in Göttingen.

BOHR. Schrödinger in Zürich, Fermi in Rome.

HEISENBERG. Chadwick and Dirac in England.

BOHR. Joliot and de Broglie in Paris.

HEISENBERG. Gamow and Landau in Russia.

BOHR. Everyone in and out of each other's departments.

HEISENBERG. Papers and drafts of papers on every international mail-train.

BOHR. You remember when Goudsmit and Uhlenbeck did spin?

HEISENBERG. There's this one last variable in the quantum state of the atom that no one can make sense of. The last hurdle.

BOHR. And these two crazy Dutchmen go back to a ridiculous idea that electrons can spin in different ways.

HEISENBERG. And of course the first thing that everyone wants to know is, What line is Copenhagen going to take?

BOHR. I'm on my way to Leiden, as it happens.

HEISENBERG. And it turns into a papal progress! The train stops on the way at Hamburg ...

BOHR. Pauli and Stern are waiting on the platform to ask me what I think about spin.

HEISENBERG. You tell them it's wrong.

BOHR. No, I tell them it's very ...

HEISENBERG. Interesting.

BOHR. I think that is precisely the word I choose.

HEISENBERG. Then the train pulls into Leiden.

BOHR. And I'm met at the barrier by Einstein and Ehrenfest. And I change my mind because Einstein - Einstein, you see? - I'm the Pope - he's God - because Einstein has made a relativistic analysis, and it resolves all my doubts.

HEISENBERG. Meanwhile I'm standing in for Max Born at Göttingen, so you make a detour there on your way home.

BOHR. And you and Jordan meet me at the station.

HEISENBERG. Same question: what do you think of spin?

BOHR. And when the train stops at Berlin there's Pauli on the platform.

HEISENBERG. Wolfgang Pauli, who never gets out of bed if he can possibly avoid it ...

BOHR. And who's already met me once at Hamburg on the journey out ...

HEISENBERG. He's traveled all the way from Hamburg to Berlin purely in order to see you for the second time round...

BOHR. And find out how my ideas on spin have developed en route.

HEISENBERG. Oh, those years! Those amazing years! Those three short years!

BOHR. From 1924 to 1927.

HEISENBERG. From when I arrived in Copenhagen to work with you.

BOHR. To when you departed, to take up your chair at Leipzig.

HEISENBERG. Three years of raw, bracing northern springtime.

BOHR. At the end of which we had quantum mechanics, we had uncertainty ...

HEISENBERG. We had complementarity ...

BOHR. We had the whole Copenhagen Interpretation.

HEISENBERG. Europe in all its glory again. A new Enlightenment, with Germany back in her rightful place at the heart of it. And who led the way for everyone else?

MARGRETHE. You and Niels.

HEISENBERG. Well, we did.

BOHR. We did.

MARGRETHE. And that's what you were trying to get back to in 1941?

HEISENBERG. To something we did in those three years... Something we said, something we thought ... I keep almost seeing it out of the corner of my eye as we talk! Something about the way we worked. Something about the way we did all those things ...

BOHR. Together.

HEISENBERG. Together. Yes, together.

MARGRETHE. No.

BOHR. No? What do you mean, no?

MARGRETHE. Not together. You didn't do any of those things together.

BOHR. Yes, we did. Of course we did.

MARGRETHE. No, you didn't. Every single one of them you did when you were apart. *You* first worked out quantum mechanics on Heligoland.

HEISENBERG. Well, it was summer by then. I had my hay fever.

MARGRETHE. And on Heligoland, on your own, on a rocky bare island in the middle of the North Sea, you said there was nothing to distract you....

HEISENBERG. My head began to clear, and I had this very sharp picture of what atomic physics ought to be like. I suddenly realized that we had to limit it to the measurements we could actually make, to what we could actually observe. We can't see the electrons inside the atom ...

MARGRETHE. Any more than Niels can see the thoughts in your head, or you the thoughts in Niels's.

HEISENBERG. All we can see are the effects that the electrons produce, on the light that they reflect.

BOHR. But the difficulties you were trying to resolve were the ones we'd explored together, over dinner in the flat, on the beach at Tisvilde.

HEISENBERG. Of course. But I remember the evening when the mathematics first began to chime with the principle.

MARGRETHE. On Heligoland

HEISENBERG. On Heligoland.

MARGRETHE. On your own.

HEISENBERG. It was terribly laborious - I didn't understand matrix calculus then ... I get so excited I keep making mistakes. But by three in the morning I've got it. I seem to be looking through the surface of atomic phenomena into a strangely beautiful interior world. A world of pure mathematical structures. I'm too excited to sleep. I go down to the southern end of the island. There's a rock jutting out into the sea that I've been longing to climb. I get up it in the half-light before the dawn, and lie on top, gazing out to sea.

MARGRETHE. On your own.

HEISENBERG. On my own. And yes - I was happy.

MARGRETHE. Happier than you were back here with us all in Copenhagen the following winter.

HEISENBERG. What, with all the Schrödinger nonsense?

BOHR. Nonsense? Come, come. Schrödinger's wave formulation?

MARGRETHE. Yes, suddenly everyone's turned their backs on your wonderful new matrix mechanics.

HEISENBERG. No one can understand it.

MARGRETHE. And they *can* understand Schrödinger's wave mechanics.

HEISENBERG. Because they'd learnt it in school! We're going backwards to classical physics! And when I'm a little cautious about accepting it...

BOHR. A little cautious? Not to criticize, but ...

MARGRETHE. ... You described it as repulsive!

HEISENBERG. I said the physical implications were repulsive. Schrödinger said my mathematics were repulsive.

BOHR. I seem to recall you used the word ... well, I won't repeat it in mixed company.

HEISENBERG. In private. But by that time people had gone crazy.

MARGRETHE. They thought you were simply jealous.

HEISENBERG. Someone even suggested some bizarre kind of intellectual snobbery. You got extremely excited.

BOHR. On your behalf.

HEISENBERG. You invited Schrödinger here ...

BOHR. To have a calm debate about our differences.

HEISENBERG. And you fell on him like a madman. You meet him at the station - of course - and you pitch into him before he's even got his bags off the train. Then you go on at him from first thing in the morning until last thing at night.

BOHR. *I* go on? *He* goes on!

HEISENBERG. Because you won't make the least concession!

BOHR. Nor will he!

HEISENBERG. You made him ill! He had to retire to bed to get away from you!

BOHR. He had a slight feverish cold.

HEISENBERG. Margrethe had to nurse him!

MARGRETHE. I dosed him with tea and cake to keep his strength up.

HEISENBERG. Yes, while you pursued him even into the sick-room! Sat on his bed and hammered away at him!

BOHR. Perfectly politely.

HEISENBERG. You were the Pope and the Holy Office and the Inquisition all rolled into one! And then, and then, after Schrödinger had fled back to Zürich - and this I will never forget, Bohr, this I will never let you forget - you started to take his side! You turned on me!

BOHR. Because *you'd* gone mad by this time! You'd become fanatical! You were refusing to allow wave theory any place in quantum mechanics at all!

HEISENBERG. You'd completely turned your coat!

BOHR. I said wave mechanics and matrix mechanics were simply alternative tools.

HEISENBERG. Something you're always accusing me of. 'If it works it works.' Never mind what it means.

BOHR. Of course I mind what it means.

HEISENBERG. What it means in language.

BOHR. In plain language, yes.

HEISENBERG. What something means is what it means in mathematics.

BOHR. You think that so long as the mathematics works out, the sense doesn't matter.

HEISENBERG. Mathematics *is* sense! That's what sense is!

BOHR. But in the end, in the end, remember, we have to be able to explain it all to Margrethe!

MARGRETHE. Explain it to me? You couldn't even explain it to each other! You went on arguing into the small hours every night! You both got so angry!

BOHR. We also both got completely exhausted.

MARGRETHE. It was the cloud chamber that finished you.

BOHR. Yes, because if you detach an electron from an atom, and send it through a cloud chamber, you can see the track it leaves.

HEISENBERG. And it's a scandal. There shouldn't be a track!

MARGRETHE. According to your quantum mechanics.

HEISENBERG. There *isn't* a track! No orbits! No tracks or trajectories! Only external effects!

MARGRETHE. Only there the track is. I've seen it myself, as clear as the wake left by a passing ship.

BOHR. It was a fascinating paradox.

HEISENBERG. You actually loved the paradoxes, that's your problem. You reveled in the contradictions.

BOHR. Yes, and you've never been able to understand the suggestiveness of paradox and contradiction. That's *your* problem. You live and breathe paradox and contradiction, but you can no more see the beauty of them than the fish can see the beauty of the water.

HEISENBERG. I sometimes felt as if I was trapped in kind of windowless hell. You don't realize how aggressive you are. Prowling up and down the room as if you're going to eat someone - and I can guess who it's going to be.

BOHR. That's the way we did the physics, though.

MARGRETHE. No. No! In the end you did it on your own again! Even you! You went off skiing in Norway.

BOHR. I had to get away from it all!

MARGRETHE. And you worked out complementarity in Norway, on your own.

HEISENBERG. The speed he skis at he had to do *something* to keep the blood going round. It was either physics or frostbite.

BOHR. Yes, and you stayed behind in Copenhagen ...

HEISENBERG. And started to think at last.

MARGRETHE. You're a lot better off apart, you two.

HEISENBERG. Having him out of town was as liberating as getting away from my hay fever on Heligoland.

MARGRETHE. I shouldn't let you sit anywhere near each other, if I were the teacher.

HEISENBERG. And that's when I did uncertainty. Walking round Faelled Park on my own one horrible raw February night. It's very late, and as soon as I've turned off into the park I'm completely alone in the darkness. I start to think about what you'd see, if you could train a telescope on me from the mountains of Norway. You'd see me by the street-lamps on the Blegdamsvej, then nothing as I vanished into the darkness, then another glimpse of me as I passed the lamppost in front of the bandstand. And that's what we see in the cloud chamber. Not a continuous track but a series of glimpses - a series of collisions between the passing electron and various molecules of water vapor ... Or think of you, on your great papal progress to Leiden in 1925. What did Margrethe see of that, at home here in Copenhagen? A picture postcard from Hamburg, perhaps. Then one from Leiden. One from Göttingen. One from Berlin. Because what we see in the cloud chamber are not even the collisions themselves, but the water droplets that condense around them, as big as cities around a traveler - no, vastly bigger still, relatively - complete countries - Germany ... Holland ... Germany again. There is no track, there are no precise addresses; only a vague list of countries visited. I don't know why we hadn't thought of it before, except that we were too busy arguing to think at all.

BOHR. You seem to have given up on all forms of discussion. By the time I get back from Norway I find you've done a draft of your uncertainty paper - and you've already sent it for publication!

MARGRETHE. And an even worse battle begins.

BOHR. My dear good Heisenberg, it's not open behavior to rush a first draft into print before we've discussed it together! It's not the way we work!

HEISENBERG. No, the way we work is that you hound me from first thing in the morning till last thing at night! The way we work is that you drive me mad!

BOHR. Yes, because the paper contains a fundamental error.

MARGRETHE. And here we go again.

HEISENBERG. No, but I show him the strangest truth about the universe that any of us has stumbled on since relativity - that you can never know everything about the whereabouts of a particle, or anything else, even Bohr now, as he prowls up and down the room in that maddening way of his, because we can't observe it without introducing some new element into the situation, a molecule of water vapor for it to hit, or a piece of light - things which have an energy of their own, and which therefore have an effect on what they hit. A small one, admittedly, in the case of Bohr ...

BOHR. Yes, if you know where I am with the kind of accuracy we're talking about when we're dealing with particles, you can still measure my velocity to within - what ...?

HEISENBERG. Something like a billionth of a billionth of a kilometer per second. The theoretical point remains, though, that you have no absolutely determinate situation in the world, which among other things lays waste to the idea of causality, the whole foundation of science - because if you don't know how things are today you certainly can't know how they're going to be tomorrow. I shatter the objective universe around you - and all you can say is that there's an error in the formulation!

BOHR. There is!

MARGRETHE. Tea, anyone? Cake?

HEISENBERG. Listen, in my paper what we're trying to locate is not a free electron off on its travels through a cloud chamber, but an electron when it's at home, moving around inside an atom ...

BOHR. And the uncertainty arises not, as you claim, through its indeterminate recoil when it's hit by an incoming photon ...

HEISENBERG. Plain language, plain language!

BOHR. This *is* plain language.

HEISENBERG. Listen ...

BOHR. The language of classical mechanics.

HEISENBERG. Listen! Copenhagen is an atom. Margrethe is its nucleus. About right, the scale? Ten thousand to one?

BOHR. Yes, yes.

HEISENBERG. Now, Bohr's an electron. He's wandering about the city somewhere in the darkness, no one knows where. He's here, he's there, he's everywhere and nowhere. Up in Faelled Park, down at

Carlsberg. Passing City Hall, out by the harbor. I'm a photon. A quantum of light. I'm dispatched into the darkness to find Bohr. And I succeed, because I manage to collide with him... But what's happened? Look - he's been slowed down, he's been deflected! He's no longer doing exactly what he was so maddeningly doing when I walked into him!

BOHR. But, Heisenberg, Heisenberg! You also have been deflected! If people can see what's happened to you, to their piece of light, then they can work out what must have happened to me! The trouble is knowing what's happened to you! Because to understand how people see you we have to treat you not just as a particle, but as a wave. I have to use not only your particle mechanics, I have to use the Schrödinger wave function.

HEISENBERG. I know - I put it in a postscript to my paper.

BOHR. Everyone remembers the paper - no one remembers the postscript. But the question is fundamental. Particles are things, complete in themselves. Waves are disturbances in something else.

HEISENBERG. I know. Complementarity. It's in the postscript.

BOHR. They're either one thing or the other. They can't be both. We have to choose one way of seeing them or the other. But as soon as we do we can't know everything about them.

HEISENBERG. And off he goes into orbit again. Incidentally exemplifying another application of complementarity. Exactly where you go as you ramble around is of course completely determined by your genes and the various physical forces acting on you. But it's also completely determined by your own entirely inscrutable whims from one moment to the next. So we can't completely understand your behavior without seeing it both ways at once, and that's impossible. Which means that your extraordinary peregrinations are not fully objective aspects of the universe. They exist only partially, through the efforts of me or Margrethe, as our minds shift endlessly back and forth between the two approaches.

BOHR. You've never absolutely and totally accepted complementarity, have you?

HEISENBERG. Yes! Absolutely and totally! I defended it at the Como Conference in 1927! I have adhered to it ever afterwards with religious fervor! You convinced me. I humbly accepted your criticisms.

BOHR. Not before you'd said some deeply wounding things.

HEISENBERG. Good God, at one point you literally reduced me to tears!

BOHR. Forgive me, but I diagnosed them as tears of frustration and rage.

HEISENBERG. I was having a tantrum?

BOHR. I have brought up children of my own.

HEISENBERG. And what about Margrethe? Was *she* having a tantrum? Klein told me you reduced *her* to tears after I'd gone, making her type out your endless redraftings of the complementarity paper.

BOHR. I don't recall that.

MARGRETHE. I do.

HEISENBERG. We had to drag Pauli out of bed in Hamburg once again to come to Copenhagen and negotiate peace.

BOHR. He succeeded. We ended up with a treaty. Uncertainty and complementarity became the two central tenets of the Copenhagen Interpretation of Quantum Mechanics.

HEISENBERG. A political compromise, of course, like most treaties.

BOHR. You see? Somewhere inside you there are still secret reservations.

HEISENBERG. Not at all - it works. That's what matters. It works, it works, it works!

BOHR. It works, yes. But it's more important than that. Because you see what we did in those three years, Heisenberg? Not to exaggerate, but we turned the world inside out! Yes, listen, now it comes, now it comes... We put man back at the center of the universe. Throughout history we keep finding ourselves displaced. We keep exiling ourselves to the periphery of things. First we turn ourselves into a mere adjunct of God's unknowable purposes, tiny figures kneeling in the great cathedral of creation. And no sooner have we recovered ourselves in the Renaissance, no sooner has man become, as Protagoras proclaimed him, the measure of all things, than we're pushed aside again by the products of our own reasoning! We're dwarfed again as physicists build the great new cathedrals for us to wonder at - the laws of classical mechanics that predate us from the beginning of eternity, that will survive us to eternity's end, that exist whether we exist or not. Until we come to the beginning of the twentieth century, and we're suddenly forced to rise from our knees again.

HEISENBERG. It starts with Einstein.

BOHR. It starts with Einstein. He shows that measurement - measurement, on which the whole possibility of science depends - measurement is not an impersonal event that occurs with impartial universality. It's a human act, carried out from a specific point of view in time and space, from the one particular viewpoint of a possible observer. Then, here in Copenhagen in those three years in the mid-twenties we discover that there is no precisely determinable objective universe. That the universe exists only as a series of approximations. Only within the limits determined by our relationship with it. Only through the understanding lodged inside the human head.

MARGRETHE. So this man you've put at the center of the universe - is it you, or is it Heisenberg?

BOHR. Now, now, my love.

MARGRETHE. Yes, but it makes a difference.

BOHR. Either of us. Both of us. Yourself. All of us.

MARGRETHE. If it's Heisenberg at the center of the universe, then the one bit of the universe that he can't see is Heisenberg.

HEISENBERG. So ...

MARGRETHE. So it's no good asking him why he came to Copenhagen in 1941. He doesn't know!

HEISENBERG. I thought for a moment just then I caught a glimpse of it.

MARGRETHE. Then you turned to look.

HEISENBERG. And away it went.

MARGRETHE. Complementarity again. Yes?

BOHR. Yes, yes.

MARGRETHE. I've typed it out often enough. If you're doing something you have to concentrate on you can't also be thinking about doing it, and if you're thinking about doing it then you can't actually be doing it. Yes?

HEISENBERG. Swerve left, swerve right, or think about it and die.

BOHR. But *after* you've done it ...

MARGRETHE. You look back and make a guess, just like the rest of us. Only a worse guess, because you didn't see yourself doing it, and we did. Forgive me, but you don't even know why you did uncertainty in the first place.

BOHR. Whereas if *you're* the one at the center of the universe ...

MARGRETHE. Then I can tell you that it was because you wanted to drop a bomb on Schrödinger.

HEISENBERG. I wanted to show he was wrong, certainly.

MARGRETHE. And Schrödinger was winning the war. When the Leipzig chair first became vacant that autumn he was short-listed for it and you weren't. You needed a wonderful new weapon.

BOHR. Not to criticize, Margrethe, but you have a tendency to make everything personal.

MARGRETHE. Because everything *is* personal! You've just read us all a lecture about it! You know how much Heisenberg wanted a chair. You know the pressure he was under from his family. I'm sorry, but you want to make everything seem heroically abstract and logical. And when you tell the story, yes, it all falls into place, it all has a beginning and a middle and an end. But I was there, and when I remember what it was like I'm there still, and I look around me and what I see isn't a story! It's confusion and rage and jealousy and tears and no one knowing what things mean or which way they're going to go.

HEISENBERG. All the same, it works, it works.

MARGRETHE. Yes, it works wonderfully. Within three months of publishing your uncertainty paper you're offered Leipzig.

HEISENBERG. I didn't mean that.

MARGRETHE. Not to mention somewhere else and somewhere else.

HEISENBERG. Halle and Munich and Zürich.

BOHR. And various American universities.

HEISENBERG. But I didn't mean that.

MARGRETHE. And when you take up your chair at Leipzig you're how old?

HEISENBERG. Twenty-six.

BOHR. The youngest full professor in Germany.

HEISENBERG. I mean the Copenhagen Interpretation. The Copenhagen Interpretation works. However we got there, by whatever combination of high principles and low calculation, of most painfully hard thought and most painfully childish tears, it works. It goes on working.

MARGRETHE. Yes, and why did you both accept the Interpretation in the end? Was it really because you wanted to re-establish humanism?

BOHR. Of course not. It was because it was the only way to explain what the experimenters had observed.

MARGRETHE. Or was it because now you were becoming a professor you wanted a solidly established doctrine to teach? Because you wanted to have your new ideas publicly endorsed by the head of the church in Copenhagen? And perhaps Niels agreed to endorse them in return for your accepting *his* doctrines. For recognizing him as head of the church. And if you want to know why you came to Copenhagen in 1941 I'll tell you that as well. You're right - there's no great mystery about it. You came to show yourself off to us.

BOHR. Margrethe!

MARGRETHE. No! When he first came in 1924 he was a humble assistant lecturer from a humiliated nation, grateful to have a job. Now here you are, back in triumph - the leading scientist in a nation that's conquered most of Europe. You've come to show us how well you've done in life.

BOHR. This is so unlike you!

MARGRETHE. I'm sorry, but isn't that really why he's here? Because he's burning to let us know that he's in charge of some vital piece of secret research. And that even so he's preserved a lofty moral independence. Preserved it so famously that he's being watched by the Gestapo. Preserved it so successfully that he's now also got a wonderfully important moral dilemma to face.

BOHR. Yes, well, now you're simply working yourself up.

MARGRETHE. A chain reaction. You tell one painful truth and it leads to two more. And as you frankly admit, you're going to go back and continue doing precisely what you were doing before, whatever Niels tells you.

HEISENBERG. Yes.

MARGRETHE. Because you wouldn't dream of giving up such a wonderful opportunity for research.

HEISENBERG. Not if I can possibly help it.

MARGRETHE. Also you want to demonstrate to the Nazis how useful theoretical physics can be. You want to save the honor of German science. You want to be there to re-establish it in all its glory as soon as the war's over.

HEISENBERG. All the same, I don't tell Speer that the reactor ...

MARGRETHE. ... will produce plutonium, no, because you're afraid of what will happen if the Nazis commit huge resources, and you fail to deliver the bombs. Please don't try to tell us that you're a hero of the resistance.

HEISENBERG. I've never claimed to be a hero.

MARGRETHE. Your talent is for skiing too fast for anyone to see where you are. For always being in more than one position at a time, like one of your particles.

HEISENBERG. I can only say that it worked. Unlike most of the gestures made by heroes of the resistance. It worked! I know what you think. You think I should have joined the plot against Hitler, and got myself hanged like the others.

BOHR. Of course not.

HEISENBERG. You don't say it, because there are some things that can't be said. But you think it.

BOHR. No.

HEISENBERG. What would it have achieved? What would it have achieved if you'd dived in after Christian, and drowned as well? But that's another thing that can't be said.

BOHR. Only thought.

HEISENBERG. Yes. I'm sorry.

BOHR. And rethought. Every day.

HEISENBERG. You had to be held back, I know.

MARGRETHE. Whereas you held yourself back.

HEISENBERG. Better to stay on the boat, though, and fetch it about. Better to remain alive, and throw the lifebuoy. Surely!

BOHR. Perhaps. Perhaps not.

HEISENBERG. Better. Better.

MARGRETHE. Really it is ridiculous. You reasoned your way, both of you, with such astonishing delicacy and precision into the tiny world of the atom. Now it turns out that everything depends upon these really rather large objects on our shoulders. And what's going on in there is ...

HEISENBERG. Elsinore.

MARGRETHE. Elsinore, yes.

HEISENBERG. And you may be right. I *was* afraid of what would happen. I *was* conscious of being on the winning side... So many explanations for everything I did! So many of them sitting round the lunch-table! Somewhere at the head of the table, I think, is the real reason I came to Copenhagen. Again I turn to look ... and for a moment I almost see its face. Then next time I look the chair at the head of the table is completely empty. There's no reason at all. I didn't tell Speer simply because I didn't think of it. I came to Copenhagen simply because I did think of it. A million things we might do or might not do every day. You see a mine - you throw a stone at it, you don't throw a stone at it. You see some ridiculous thing to climb - you don't climb it, you do climb it. A million decisions that make themselves. Why didn't you kill me?

BOHR. Why didn't I ...?

HEISENBERG. Kill me. Murder me. That evening in 1941. Here we are, walking back towards the house, and you've just leapt to the conclusion that I'm going to arm Hitler with nuclear weapons. You'll surely take any reasonable steps to prevent it happening.

BOHR. By murdering you?

HEISENBERG. We're in the middle of a war. I'm an enemy. There's nothing odd or immoral about killing enemies.

BOHR. I should fetch out my cap pistol?

HEISENBERG. You won't need your cap pistol. You won't even need a mine. You can do it without any loud bangs, without any blood, without any spectacle of suffering. As cleanly as a bomb aimer pressing his release three thousand meters above the earth. You simply wait till I've gone. Then you sit quietly down in your favorite armchair here and repeat aloud to Margrethe, in front of our unseen audience, what I've just told you. I shall be dead almost as soon as poor Casimir. A lot sooner than Gamow.

BOHR. My dear Heisenberg, the suggestion is of course ...

HEISENBERG. Most interesting. So interesting that it never even occurred to you. Complementarity, once again. I'm your enemy;

I'm also your friend. I'm a danger to mankind; I'm also your guest. I'm a particle; I'm also a wave. We have one set of obligations to the world in general, and we have other sets, never to be reconciled, to our fellow-countrymen, to our neighbors, to our friends, to our family, to our children. We have to go through not two slits at the same time but twenty-two. All we can do is to look afterwards, and see what happened.

MARGRETHE. I'll tell you another reason why you did uncertainty: you have a natural affinity for it.

HEISENBERG. Well, I must cut a gratifyingly chastened figure when I return in 1947. Crawling on my hands and knees again. My nation back in ruins.

MARGRETHE. Not really. You're demonstrating that once more you personally have come out on top.

HEISENBERG. Begging for food parcels?

MARGRETHE. Established in Göttingen under British protection, in charge of post-war German science.

HEISENBERG. That first year in Göttingen I slept on straw.

MARGRETHE. Elisabeth said you had a most charming house thereafter.

HEISENBERG. I was given it by the British.

MARGRETHE. Your new foster parents. Who'd confiscated it from someone else.

BOHR. Enough, my love, enough.

MARGRETHE. No, I've kept my thoughts to myself for all these years. But it's maddening to have this clever son forever dancing about in front of our eyes, forever demanding our approval, forever struggling to shock us, forever begging to be told what the limits to his freedom are, if only so that he can go out and transgress them! I'm sorry, but really.... On your hands and knees? It's my dear, good, kind husband who's on his hands and knees! Literally. Crawling down to the beach in the darkness in 1943, fleeing like a thief in the night from his own homeland to escape being murdered. The protection of the German Embassy that you boasted about didn't last for long. We were incorporated into the Reich.

HEISENBERG. I warned you in 1941. You wouldn't listen. At least Bohr got across to Sweden.

MARGRETHE. And even as the fishing-boat was taking him across the Sound two freighters were arriving in the harbor to ship the entire Jewish population of Denmark eastwards. That great darkness inside the human soul was flooding out to engulf us all.

HEISENBERG. I did try to warn you.

MARGRETHE. Yes, and where are you? Shut away in a cave like a savage, trying to conjure an evil spirit out of a hole in the ground. That's what it came down to in the end, all that shining springtime in the 1920s, that's what it produced - a more efficient machine for killing people.

BOHR. It breaks my heart every time I think of it.

HEISENBERG. It broke all our hearts.

MARGRETHE. And this wonderful machine may yet kill every man, woman, and child in the world. And if we really are the center of the universe, if we really are all that's keeping it in being, what will be left?

BOHR. Darkness. Total and final darkness.

MARGRETHE. Even the questions that haunt us will at last be extinguished. Even the ghosts will die.

HEISENBERG. I can only say that I didn't do it. I didn't build the bomb.

MARGRETHE. No, and why didn't you? I'll tell you that, too. It's the simplest reason of all. Because you couldn't. You didn't understand the physics.

HEISENBERG. That's what Goudsmit said.

MARGRETHE. And Goudsmit knew. He was one of your magic circle. He and Uhlenbeck were the ones who did spin.

HEISENBERG. All the same, he had no idea of what I did or didn't understand about a bomb.

MARGRETHE. He tracked you down across Europe for Allied Intelligence. He interrogated you after you were captured.

HEISENBERG. He blamed me, of course. His parents died in Auschwitz. He thought I should have done something to save them. I don't know what. So many hands stretching up from the darkness for a lifeline, and no lifeline that could ever reach them ...

MARGRETHE. He said you didn't understand the crucial difference between a reactor and a bomb.

HEISENBERG. I understood very clearly. I simply didn't tell the others.

MARGRETHE. Ah.

HEISENBERG. I understood, though.

MARGRETHE. But secretly.

HEISENBERG. You can check if you don't believe me.

MARGRETHE. There's evidence, for once?

HEISENBERG. It was all most carefully recorded.

MARGRETHE. Witnesses, even?

HEISENBERG. Unimpeachable witnesses.

MARGRETHE. Who wrote it down?

HEISENBERG. Who recorded it and transcribed it.

MARGRETHE. Even though you didn't tell anyone?

HEISENBERG. I told one person. I told Otto Hahn. That terrible night at Farm Hall, after we'd heard the news. Somewhere in the small hours, after everyone had finally gone to bed, and we were alone together. I gave him a reasonably good account of how the bomb had worked.

MARGRETHE. After the event.

HEISENBERG. After the event. Yes. When it didn't matter any more. All the things Goudsmit said I didn't understand. Fast neutrons in 235. The plutonium option. A reflective shell to reduce neutron escape. Even the method of triggering it.

BOHR. The critical mass. That was the most important thing. The amount of material you needed to establish the chain reaction. Did you tell him the critical mass?

HEISENBERG. I gave him a figure, yes. You can look it up! Because that was the other secret of the house party. Diebner asked me when we first arrived if I thought there were hidden microphones. I laughed. I told him the British were far too old-fashioned to know about Gestapo methods. I underestimated them. They had microphones everywhere - they were recording everything. Look it up! Everything we said. Everything we went through that terrible night. Everything I told Hahn alone in the small hours.

BOHR. But the critical mass. You gave him a figure. What was the figure you gave him?

HEISENBERG. I forget.

BOHR. Heisenberg ...

HEISENBERG. It's all on the record. You can see for yourself.

BOHR. The figure for the Hiroshima bomb ...

HEISENBERG. Was fifty kilograms.

BOHR. So that was that the figure you gave Hahn? Fifty kilograms?

HEISENBERG. I said about a ton.

BOHR. About a ton? A thousand kilograms? Heisenberg, I believe I am at last beginning to understand something.

HEISENBERG. The one thing I was wrong about.

BOHR. You were twenty times over.

HEISENBERG. The one thing.

BOHR. But, Heisenberg, your mathematics, your mathematics! How could they have been so far out?

HEISENBERG. They weren't. As soon as I calculated the diffusion I got it just about right.

BOHR. As soon as you calculated it?

HEISENBERG. I gave everyone a seminar on it a week later. It's in the record! Look it up!

BOHR. You mean ... you hadn't calculated it before? You hadn't done the diffusion equation?

HEISENBERG. There was no need to.

BOHR. No need to?

HEISENBERG. The calculation had already been done.

BOHR. Done by whom?

HEISENBERG. By Perrin and Flügge in 1939.

BOHR. By Perrin and Flügge? But, my dear Heisenberg, that was for natural uranium. Wheeler and I showed that it was only the 235 that fissioned.

HEISENBERG. Your great paper. The basis of everything we did.

BOHR. So you needed to calculate the figure for pure 235.

HEISENBERG. Obviously.

BOHR. And you didn't?

HEISENBERG. I didn't.

BOHR. And that's why you were so confident you couldn't do it until you had the plutonium. Because you spent the entire war believing that it would take not a few kilograms of 235, but a ton or more. And to make a ton of 235 in any plausible time ...

HEISENBERG. Would have needed something like two hundred million separator units. It was plainly unimaginable.

BOHR If you'd realized you had to produce only a few kilograms ...

HEISENBERG. Even to make a single kilogram would need something like two hundred thousand units.

BOHR. But two hundred million is one thing; two hundred thousand is another. You might just possibly have imagined setting up two hundred thousand.

HEISENBERG. Just possibly.

BOHR. The Americans did imagine it.

HEISENBERG. Because Otto Frisch and Rudolf Peierls actually did the calculation. They solved the diffusion equation.

BOHR. Frisch was my old assistant.

HEISENBERG. Peierls was my old pupil.

BOHR. An Austrian and a German.

HEISENBERG. So they should have been making their calculation for us, at the Kaiser Wilhelm Institute in Berlin. But instead they made it at the University of Birmingham, in England.

MARGRETHE. Because they were Jews.

HEISENBERG. There's something almost mathematically elegant about that.

BOHR. They also started with Perrin and Flügge.

HEISENBERG. They also thought it would take tons. They also thought it was unimaginable.

BOHR. Until one day ...

HEISENBERG. They did the calculation.

BOHR. They discovered just how fast the chain reaction would go.

HEISENBERG. And therefore how little material you'd need.

BOHR. They said slightly over half a kilogram.

HEISENBERG. About the size of a tennis ball.

BOHR. They were wrong, of course.

HEISENBERG. They were a hundred times under.

BOHR. Which made it seem a hundred times more imaginable

than it actually was.

HEISENBERG. Whereas I left it seeming twenty times less imaginable.

BOHR. So all your agonizing in Copenhagen about plutonium was beside the point. You could have done it without ever building the reactor. You could have done it with 235 all the time.

HEISENBERG. Almost certainly not.

BOHR. Just possibly, though.

HEISENBERG. Just possibly.

BOHR. And *that* question you'd settled long before you arrived in Copenhagen. Simply by failing to try the diffusion equation.

HEISENBERG. Such a tiny failure.

BOHR. But the consequences went branching out over the years, doubling and redoubling.

HEISENBERG. Until they were large enough to save a city. Which city? Any of the cities that we never dropped our bomb on.

BOHR. London, presumably, if you'd had it in time. If the Americans had already entered the war, and the Allies had begun to liberate Europe, then ...

HEISENBERG. Who knows? Paris as well. Amsterdam. Perhaps Copenhagen.

BOHR. So, Heisenberg, tell us this one simple thing: why didn't you do the calculation?

HEISENBERG. The question is why Frisch and Peierls *did* do it. It was a stupid waste of time. However much 235 it turned out to be, it was obviously going to be more than anyone could imagine producing.

BOHR. Except that it wasn't!

HEISENBERG. Except that it wasn't.

BOHR. So why ...?

HEISENBERG. I don't know! I don't know why I didn't do it! Because I never thought of it! Because it didn't occur to me! Because I assumed it wasn't worth doing!

BOHR. Assumed? Assumed? You never assumed things! That's how you got uncertainty, because you rejected our assumptions! You calculated, Heisenberg! You calculated everything! The first thing you did with a problem was the mathematics!

HEISENBERG. You should have been there to slow me down.

BOHR. Yes, you wouldn't have got away with it if I'd been standing over you.

HEISENBERG. Though in fact you made exactly the same assumption! You thought there was no danger for exactly the same reason as I did! Why didn't *you* calculate it?

BOHR. Why didn't *I* calculate it?

HEISENBERG. Tell us why *you* didn't calculate it and we'll know why *I* didn't!

BOHR. It's obvious why *I* didn't!

HEISENBERG. Go on.

MARGRETHE. Because he wasn't trying to build a bomb!

HEISENBERG. Yes. Thank you. Because he wasn't trying to build a bomb. I imagine it was the same with me. Because *I* wasn't trying to build a bomb. Thank you.

BOHR. So, you bluffed yourself, the way I did at poker with the straight I never had. But in that case ...

HEISENBERG. Why did I come to Copenhagen? Yes, why did I come ...?

BOHR. One more draft, yes? One final draft!

HEISENBERG. And once again I crunch over the familiar gravel to the Bohrs' front door, and tug at the familiar bell pull. Why have I come? I know perfectly well. Know so well that I've no need to ask myself. Until once again the heavy front door opens.

BOHR. He stands on the doorstep blinking in the sudden flood of light from the house. Until this instant his thoughts have been everywhere and nowhere, like unobserved particles, through all the slits in the diffraction grating simultaneously. Now they have to be observed and specified.

HEISENBERG. And at once the clear purposes inside my head lose all definite shape. The light falls on them and they scatter.

BOHR. My dear Heisenberg!

HEISENBERG. My dear Bohr!

BOHR. Come in, come in ...

HEISENBERG. How difficult it is to see even what's in front of one's eyes. All we possess is the present, and the present endlessly dissolves into the past. Bohr has gone even as I turn to see Margrethe.

MARGRETHE. Niels is right. You look older.

BOHR. I believe you had some personal trouble.

HEISENBERG. Margrethe slips into history even as I turn back to Bohr. And yet how much more difficult still it is to catch the slightest glimpse of what's behind one's eyes. Here I am at the center of the universe, and yet all I can see are two smiles that don't belong to me.

MARGRETHE. How is Elisabeth? How are the children?

HEISENBERG. Very well. They send their love, of course... I can feel a third smile in the room, very close to me. Could it be the one I suddenly see for a moment in the mirror there? And is the awkward stranger wearing it in any way connected with this presence that I can feel in the room? This all-enveloping unobserved presence?

MARGRETHE. I watch the two smiles in the room, one awkward and ingratiating, the other rapidly fading from incautious warmth to bare politeness. There's also a third smile in the room, I know, unchangingly courteous, I hope, and unchangingly guarded.

HEISENBERG. You've managed to get some skiing?

BOHR. I glance at Margrethe, and for a moment I see what she can see and I can't - myself, and the smile vanishing from my face as poor Heisenberg blunders on.

HEISENBERG. I look at the two of them looking at me, and for a moment I see the third person in the room as clearly as I see them. Their importunate guest, stumbling from one crass and unwelcome thoughtfulness to the next.

BOHR. I look at him looking at me, anxiously, pleadingly, urging me back to the old days, and I see what he sees. And yes - now it comes, now it comes - there's someone missing from the room. He sees me. He sees Margrethe. He doesn't see himself.

HEISENBERG. Two thousand million people in the world, and the one who has to decide their fate is the only one who's always hidden from me.

BOHR. You suggested a stroll.

HEISENBERG. You remember Elsinore? The darkness inside the human soul ...?

BOHR. And out we go. Out under the autumn trees. Through the blacked-out streets.

HEISENBERG. Now there's no one in the world except Bohr

and the invisible other. Who is he, this all-enveloping presence in the darkness?

MARGRETHE. The flying particle wanders the darkness, no one knows where. It's here, it's there, it's everywhere and nowhere.

BOHR. With careful casualness he begins to ask the question he's prepared.

HEISENBERG. Does one as a physicist have the moral right to work on the practical exploitation of atomic energy?

MARGRETHE. The great collision.

BOHR. I stop. He stops ...

MARGRETHE. This is how they work.

HEISENBERG. He gazes at me, horrified.

MARGRETHE. Now at last he knows where he is and what he's doing.

HEISENBERG. He turns away.

MARGRETHE. And even as the moment of collision begins it's over.

BOHR. Already we're hurrying back towards the house.

MARGRETHE. Already they're both flying away from each other into the darkness again.

HEISENBERG. Our conversation's over.

BOHR. Our great partnership.

HEISENBERG. All our friendship.

MARGRETHE. And everything about him becomes as uncertain as it was before.

BOHR. Unless ... yes ... a thought-experiment... Let's suppose for a moment that I don't go flying off into the night. Let's see what happens if instead I remember the paternal role I'm supposed to play. If I stop, and control my anger, and turn to him. And ask him why.

HEISENBERG. Why?

BOHR. Why are you confident that it's going to be so reassuringly difficult to build a bomb with 235? Is it because you've done the calculation?

HEISENBERG. The calculation?

BOHR. Of the diffusion in 235. No. It's because you haven't calculated it. You haven't considered calculating it. You hadn't consciously realized there was a calculation to be made.

HEISENBERG. And of course now I *have* realized. In fact it wouldn't be all that difficult. Let's see... The scattering cross-section's about 6 x 10^{-24}, so the mean free path would be... Hold on ...

BOHR. And suddenly a very different and very terrible new world begins to take shape ...

MARGRETHE. That was the last and greatest demand that Heisenberg made on his friendship with you. To be understood when he couldn't understand himself. And that was the last and greatest act of friendship for Heisenberg that you performed in return. To leave him misunderstood.

HEISENBERG. Yes. Perhaps I should thank you.

BOHR. Perhaps you should.

MARGRETHE. Anyway, it was the end of the story.

BOHR. Though perhaps there was also something I should thank *you* for. That summer night in 1943, when I escaped across the Sound in the fishing boat, and the freighters arrived from Germany ...

MARGRETHE, What's that to do with Heisenberg?

BOHR. When the ships arrived on the Wednesday there were eight thousand Jews in Denmark to be arrested and crammed into their holds. The following day, on the eve of the Jewish New Year, when the SS began their round-up, there was scarcely a Jew to be found.

MARGRETHE. They'd all been hidden in churches and hospitals, in people's homes and country cottages.

BOHR. But how was that possible? - Because we'd been tipped off by someone in the German Embassy.

HEISENBERG. Georg Duckwitz, their shipping specialist.

BOHR. Your man?

HEISENBERG. One of them.

BOHR. He was a remarkable informant. He told us the day before the freighters arrived - the very day that Hitler issued the order. He gave us the exact time that the SS would move.

MARGRETHE. It was the Resistance who got them out of their hiding places and smuggled them across the Sound.

BOHR. For a handful of us in one fishing smack to get past the German patrol boats was remarkable enough. For a whole armada to get past, with the best part of eight thousand people on board, was like the Red Sea parting.

MARGRETHE. I thought there *were* no German patrol boats that night?

BOHR. No - the whole squadron had suddenly been reported unseaworthy.

HEISENBERG. How they got away with it I can't imagine.

BOHR. Duckwitz again?

HEISENBERG. He also went to Stockholm and asked the Swedish government to accept everyone.

BOHR. So perhaps I should thank you.

HEISENBERG. For what?

BOHR. My life. All our lives.

HEISENBERG. Nothing to do with me by that time. I regret to say.

BOHR. But after I'd gone you came back to Copenhagen.

HEISENBERG. To make sure that our people didn't take over the Institute in your absence.

BOHR. I've never thanked you for that, either.

HEISENBERG. You know they offered me your cyclotron?

BOHR. You could have separated a little 235 with it.

HEISENBERG. Meanwhile you were going on from Sweden to Los Alamos.

BOHR. To play my small but helpful part in the deaths of a hundred thousand people.

MARGRETHE. Niels, you did nothing wrong!

BOHR. Didn't I?

HEISENBERG. Of course not. You were a good man, from first to last, and no one could ever say otherwise. Whereas I ...

BOHR. Whereas you, my dear Heisenberg, never managed to contribute to the death of one single solitary person in all your life.

MARGRETHE. Well, yes.

HEISENBERG. Did I?

MARGRETHE. One. Or so you told us. The poor fellow you guarded overnight, when you were a boy in Munich, while he was waiting to be shot in the morning.

BOHR. All right, then, one. One single soul on his conscience, to set against all the others.

MARGRETHE. But that one single soul was emperor of the universe, no less than each of us. Until the morning came.

HEISENBERG. No, when the morning came I persuaded them to let him go.

BOHR. Heisenberg, I have to say - if people are to be measured strictly in terms of observable quantities ...

HEISENBERG. Then we should need a strange new quantum ethics. There'd be a place in heaven for me. And another one for the SS man I met on my way home from Haigerloch. That was the end of my war. The Allied troops were closing in; there was nothing more we could do. Elisabeth and the children had taken refuge in a village in Bavaria, so I went to see them before I was captured. I had to go by bicycle - there were no trains or road transport by that time - and I had to travel by night and sleep under a hedge by day, because all through the daylight hours the skies were full of Allied planes, scouring the roads for anything that moved. A man on a bicycle would have been the biggest target left in Germany. Three days and three nights I traveled. Out of Württemberg, down through the Swabian Jura and the first foothills of the Alps. Across my ruined homeland. Was this what I'd chosen for it? This endless rubble? This perpetual smoke in the sky? These hungry faces? Was this my doing? And all the desperate people on the roads. The most desperate of all were the SS. Bands of fanatics with nothing left to lose, roaming around shooting deserters out of hand, hanging them from roadside trees. The second night, and suddenly there it is - the terrible familiar black tunic emerging from the twilight in front of me. On his lips as I stop - the one terrible familiar word. 'Deserter,' he says. He sounds as exhausted as I am. I give him the travel order I've written for myself. But there's hardly enough light in the sky to read by, and he's too weary to bother. He begins to open his holster instead. He's going to shoot me because it's simply less labor. And suddenly I'm thinking very quickly and clearly - it's like skiing, or that night on Heligoland, or the one in Faelled Park. What comes into my mind this time is the pack of American cigarettes I've got in my pocket. And already it's in my hand - I'm holding it out to him. The most desperate solution to a problem yet. I wait while he stands there looking at it, trying to make it out, trying to think, his left hand holding my useless piece of paper, his right on the fastening of the holster. There are two simple words in large print on the pack: Lucky Strike. He closes the holster, and takes the cigarettes instead... It had worked, it had worked! Like all the other solutions to all the other problems. For twenty cigarettes he let me live. And on I went. Three days and three nights. Past the weeping children, the lost and hungry children, drafted to fight, then abandoned by their commanders. Past the starving slave-laborers walking home to France, to Poland, to Estonia. Through Gammertingen and Biberach and Memmingen. Mindelheim, Kaufbeuren, and Schöngau. Across my beloved homeland. My ruined and dishonored and beloved homeland.

BOHR. My dear Heisenberg! My dear friend!

MARGRETHE. Silence. The silence we always in the end return to.

HEISENBERG. And of course I know what they're thinking about.

MARGRETHE. All those lost children on the road.

BOHR. Heisenberg wandering the world like a lost child himself.

MARGRETHE. Our own lost children.

HEISENBERG. And over goes the tiller once again.

BOHR. So near, so near! So slight a thing!

MARGRETHE. He stands in the doorway, watching me, then he turns his head away ...

HEISENBERG. And once again away he goes, into the dark waters.

BOHR. Before we can lay our hands on anything, our life's over.

HEISENBERG. Before we can glimpse who or what we are, we're gone and laid to dust.

BOHR. Settled among all the dust we raised.

MARGRETHE. And sooner or later there will come a time when all our children are laid to dust, and all our children's children.

BOHR. When no more decisions, great or small, are ever made again. When there's no more uncertainty, because there's no more knowledge.

MARGRETHE. And when all our eyes are closed, when even the ghosts have gone, what will be left of our beloved world? Our ruined and dishonored and beloved world?

HEISENBERG. But in the meanwhile, in this most precious meanwhile, there it is. The trees in Faelled Park. Gammertingen and Biberach and Mindelheim. Our children and our children's children. Preserved, just possibly, by that one short moment in Copenhagen. By some event that will never quite be located or defined. By that final core of uncertainty at the heart of things.

POSTSCRIPT

Where a work of fiction features historical characters and historical events it's reasonable to want to know how much of it is fiction and how much of it is history. So let me make it as clear as I can in regard to this play.

The central event in it is a real one. Heisenberg *did* go to Copenhagen in 1941, and there *was* a meeting with Bohr, in the teeth of all the difficulties encountered by my characters. He probably went to dinner at the Bohrs' house, and the two men probably went for a walk to escape from any possible microphones, though there is some dispute about even these simple matters. The question of what they actually said to each other has been even more disputed, and where there's ambiguity in the play about what happened, it's because there is in the recollection of the participants. Much more sustained speculation still has been devoted to the question of what Heisenberg was hoping to achieve by the meeting. All the alternative and co-existing explications offered in the play, except perhaps the final one, have been aired at various times, in one form or another.

Most anxious of all to establish some agreed version of the meeting was Heisenberg himself. He did indeed go back in 1947 with his British minder, Ronald Fraser, and attempted to find some common ground in the matter with Bohr. But it proved to be too delicate a task, and (according to Heisenberg, at any rate, in his memoirs) 'we both came to feel that it would be better to stop disturbing the spirits of the past.' This is where my play departs from the historical record, by supposing that at some later time, when everyone involved had become spirits of the past themselves, they argued the question out further, until they had achieved a little more understanding of what was going on, just as they had so many times when they were alive with the intractable difficulties presented by the internal workings of the atom.

The account of these earlier discussions in the twenties reflects at any rate one or two of the key topics, and the passion with which the argument was conducted, as it emerges from the biographical and autobiographical record. I am acutely aware of how over-simplified my version is. Max Born described the real story as not so much 'a

straight staircase upwards, but a tangle of interconnected alleys,' and I
have found it impossible to follow these in any detail (even where I
can begin to understand them). In particular I have grossly understated
the crucial role played by Born himself and by his pupil Pascual Jordan at Göttingen in formulating quantum mechanics (it was Born who
supplied the understanding of matrices that Heisenberg lacked, and
the statistical interpretation of Schrödinger's wave function), and of
Wolfgang Pauli in Hamburg, whose exclusion principle filled in one
of the key pieces in the puzzle.

But the account of the German and American bomb programs,
and of the two physicists' participation in them, is taken from the historical record; so is the fate of Danish Jewry; Heisenberg's experi-
ences in Germany before and during the war, his subsequent internment, and the depression that clouded his later years. I have filled out
some of the details, but in general what he says happened to him - at
the end of the First World War, on Heligoland, during his nocturnal
walk in Faelled Park, during the Berlin air-raid and his internment,
and on his ride across Germany, with its near-fatal encounter along
the way - is based very closely upon the accounts he gave in life.

The actual words spoken by my characters are of course entirely
their own. If this needs any justification then I can only appeal to Heisenberg himself. In his memoirs dialogue plays an important part, he
says, because he hopes 'to demonstrate that science is rooted in conversations.' But, as he explains, conversations, even real conversations, cannot be reconstructed literally several decades later. So he
freely reinvents them, and appeals in his turn to Thucydides.
(Heisenberg's father was a professor of classics, and he was an accomplished classicist himself, on top of all his other distinctions.)
Thucydides explains in his preface to the *History of the Peloponne-
sian War* that, although he had avoided all 'storytelling,' when it came
to the speeches, 'I have found it impossible to remember their exact
wording. Hence I have made each orator speak as, in my opinion, he
would have done in the circumstances, but keeping as close as I could
to the train of thought that guided his actual speech.' Thucydides was
trying to give an account of speeches that had actually been made,
many of which he had himself heard. Some of the dialogue in my play
represents speeches that must have been made in one form or another;

some of it speeches that were certainly never made at all. I hope, though, that in some sense it respects the Thucydidean principle, and that speeches (and indeed actions) follow in so far as possible the original protagonists' train of thought.

But how far is it possible to know what their train of thought was? This is where I have departed from the established historical record - from any possible historical record. The great challenge facing the storyteller and the historian alike is to get inside people's heads, to stand where they stood and see the world as they saw it, to make some informed estimate of their motives and intentions - and this is precisely where recorded and recordable history cannot reach. Even when all the external evidence has been mastered, the only way into the protagonists' heads is through the imagination. This indeed is the substance of the play.

*

I can't claim to be the first person to notice the parallels between Heisenberg's science and his life. They provide David Cassidy with the title (*Uncertainty*) for his excellent biography (the standard work in English). 'Especially difficult and controversial,' says Cassidy in his introduction, 'is a retrospective evaluation of Heisenberg's activities during the Third Reich and particularly during World War II. Since the end of the war, an enormous range of views about this man and his behavior have been expressed, views that have been fervently, even passionately, held by a variety of individuals. It is as if, for some, the intense emotions unleashed by the unspeakable horrors of that war and regime have combined with the many ambiguities, dualities, and compromises of Heisenberg's life and actions to make Heisenberg himself subject to a type of uncertainty principle ...' Thomas Powers makes a similar point in his extraordinary and encyclopedic book *Heisenberg's War*, which first aroused my interest in the trip to Copenhagen; he says that Heisenberg's later reticence on his role in the failure of the German bomb program 'introduces an element of irreducible uncertainty.'

Cassidy does not explore the parallel further. Powers even appends a footnote to his comment: 'Forgive me.' The apology seems to me unnecessary. It's true that the concept of uncertainty is one of those scientific notions that has become common coinage, and generalized to the point of losing much of its original meaning. The idea as introduced by Heisenberg into quantum mechanics was precise and technical. It didn't suggest that everything about the behavior of particles was unknowable, or hazy. What it limited was the simultaneous measurement of 'canonically conjugate variables,' such as position and momentum, or energy and time. The more precisely you measure one variable, it said, the less precise your measurement of the related variable can be; and this ratio, the uncertainty relationship, is itself precisely formulable.

None of this, plainly, applies directly to our observations of thought and intention. Thoughts are not locatable by pairs of conjugate variables, so there can be no question of a ratio of precision. Powers seems to imply that in Heisenberg's case the uncertainty arises purely because 'questions of motive and intention cannot be established more clearly than he was willing to state them.' It's true that Heisenberg was under contradictory pressures after the war which made it particularly difficult for him to explain what he had been trying to do. He wanted to distance himself from the Nazis, but he didn't want to suggest that he had been a traitor. He was reluctant to claim to his fellow-Germans that he had deliberately lost them the war, but he was no less reluctant to suggest that he had failed them simply out of incompetence.

But the uncertainty surely begins long before the point where Heisenberg might have offered an explanation. He was under at least as many contradictory pressures at the time to shape the actions he later failed to explain, and the uncertainty would still have existed, for us and for him, even if he had been as open, honest, and helpful as it is humanly possible to be. What people say about their own motives and intentions, even when they are not caught in the traps that entangled Heisenberg, is always subject to question - as subject to question as what anybody else says about them. Thoughts and intentions, even one's own - perhaps one's own most of all - remain shifting and elusive. There is not one single thought or intention of any sort that can ever be precisely established.

What the uncertainty of thoughts does have in common with the uncertainty of particles is that the difficulty is not just a practical one, but a systematic limitation which cannot even in theory be circumvented. It is patently not resolved by the efforts of psychologists and psycho-analysts, and it will not be resolved by neurologists, either, even when everything is known about the structure and workings of the brain, any more than semantic questions can be resolved by looking at the machine code of a computer. And since, according to the so-called 'Copenhagen Interpretation' of quantum mechanics - the interconnected set of theories that was developed by Heisenberg, Bohr, and others in the twenties - the whole possibility of saying or thinking anything about the world, even the most apparently objective, abstract aspects of it studied by the natural sciences, depends upon human observation, and is subject to the limitations which the human mind imposes, this uncertainty in our thinking is also fundamental to the nature of the world.

'Uncertainty' is not a very satisfactory word to come at this. It sits awkwardly even in its original context. You can be uncertain about things which are themselves entirely definite, and about which you could be entirely certain if you were simply better informed. Indeed, the very idea of uncertainty seems to imply the possibility of certainty. Heisenberg and Bohr used several different German words in different contexts. Bohr (who spoke more or less perfect German) sometimes referred to *Unsicherheit*, which means quite simply unsureness. In Heisenberg's original paper he talks about *Ungenauigkeit* - inexactness - and the most usual term now in German seems to be *Unschärfe* - blurredness or fuzziness. But the word he adopts in his general conclusion, and which he uses when he refers back to the period later in his memoirs, is *Unbestimmtheit*, for which it's harder to find a satisfactory English equivalent. Although it means uncertainty in the sense of vagueness, it's plainly derived from *bestimmen*, to determine or to ascertain. This is reflected better in the other English translation which is sometimes used, but which seems to be less familiar: indeterminacy. 'Undeterminedness' would be closer still, though clumsy. Less close to the German, but even closer to the reality of the situation, would be 'indeterminability'.

Questions of translation apart, Heisenberg's choice of word suggests that, at the time he wrote his paper, he had not fully grasped the metaphysical implications of what he was saying. Indeed, he concludes that the experiments concerned are affected by *Unbestimmtheit* 'purely empirically.' He was not, as Bohr complained, at that time greatly interested in the philosophical fallout from physics and mathematics (though he became much more so later on in life), and he was publishing in a hurry, as Bohr also complained, before he had had a chance to discuss the work with either Bohr or anyone else. His paper seems to imply that electrons have definite orbits, even if these are unknowable; he talks about a quantum of light completely throwing the electron out of its 'orbit,' even though he puts the word into inverted commas, and says that it has no rational sense here. The title of the paper itself reinforces this impression: *Über den anschaulichen Inhalt der quantentheoretischen Kinematik und Mechanik*. Again there are translation problems. '*Anschaulich*' means graphic, concrete, 'look-at-able'; the title is usually translated as referring to the 'perceptual' content of the disciplines concerned, which again seems to suggest a contrast with their unperceived aspects - as if Heisenberg were concerned merely about our difficulties in visualizing abstractions, not about the physical implications of this.

*

The Copenhagen Interpretation of quantum mechanics was scientific orthodoxy for most of the twentieth century, and is the theoretical basis (for better or worse) on which the century's dramatic physical demonstrations of nuclear forces were constructed. But it has not gone unchallenged. Einstein never accepted it, though he could never find a way round it. The mathematician Roger Penrose regards the present state of quantum theory as 'provisional,' and quotes Schrödinger, de Broglie, and Dirac as forerunners in this view.

An alternative to the Copenhagen Interpretation, explaining the apparent superimposition of different states that appears at the quantum level in terms of a multiplicity of parallel worlds, was developed after the Second World War by Hugh Everett III, who had been a graduate student of John Wheeler, Bohr's associate in the famous paper which opened the way to an understanding of uranium fission. David Deutsch, who proposes an extreme version of Everett's ideas in

his book *The Fabric of Reality*, claims that 'hardly anyone' still believes in the Copenhagen Interpretation. I have put this view to a number of physicists. They all seemed greatly surprised by it; but maybe I
have hit upon precisely the supposed handful who remain in the faith.

Another follower of Everett (though he seems to differ quite
sharply from Deutsch) is Murray Gell-Mann, who with Yuval
Ne'eman revolutionized elementary particle theory in the sixties with
the introduction of the quark, in its three different 'colors' and six different 'flavors,' as the fundamental unit of the material world. Gell-
Mann believes that quantum mechanics is the fundamental tool for
understanding the universe, but he sees the Copenhagen Interpretation, with its dependence upon an observer and the human act of
measurement, as anthropocentric, and as characterizing merely a special case that he calls 'the approximate quantum mechanics of measured systems.' I hesitate to express any reservations about something I
understand so little, particularly when it comes from such an authority, but it seems to me that the view which Gell-Mann favors, and
which involves what he calls alternative 'histories' or 'narratives,' is
precisely as anthropocentric as Bohr's, since histories and narratives
are not freestanding elements of the universe, but human constructs as
subjective and as restricted in their viewpoint as the act of observation.

The relevance of indeterminacy to quantum mechanics has also
been challenged. A version of the famous thought experiment involv-
ing two slits has now actually been carried out in the laboratory (at the
University of Konstanz). It confirms, as Bohr hypothesized, that while
an unobserved particle seems to pass through both slits, so that it
forms a characteristic interference pattern on a screen beyond them,
any act of observation that attempts to determine which of the two
paths the particle actually follows necessarily destroys the phenomenon, so that the interference pattern vanishes. But the experiment appears to suggest that, although the uncertainty principle is true, it accounts for discrepancies far too small to explain the loss of interference. The observation in the laboratory experiment, moreover, was
carried out not, as in the old thought experiment, by hitting the particle involved with a photon, which transfers part of its energy to the
particle and so alters its path, but by a way of marking with micro-

waves which has almost no effect on the particle's momentum.

Some physicists now accept that the loss of interference is caused by a much stranger and less quasi-classical aspect of the quantum world - entanglement. The notion was introduced by Schrödinger in 1935, and suggests that where quantum-mechanical entities become involved with each other (as with the particle and the photon), they form states of affairs which continue to have a collective identity and behavior, even though their components have physically separated again. The difficulties in this are obvious, but there is no interpretation of quantum-mechanical phenomena that does not involve breathtaking challenges to the logic of our everyday experience.

For the references to all these developments see the bibliography at the end of this Postscript.

*

What about my characters? Are they anything like their originals?

It's impossible to catch the exact tone of voice of people one never knew, with only the written record to go on, especially when most of what their contemporaries recall them as saying was originally said in other languages. There are also more particular problems with all three of my protagonists.

Bohr, for a start, was as notorious for his inarticulacy and inaudibility as he was famous for his goodness and lovability. He was fluent in various languages, but I have heard it said that the problem was to know which language he was being fluent in. Schrödinger, after his epic confrontation with Bohr in 1926, described him as often talking 'for minutes almost in a dreamlike, visionary and really quite unclear manner, partly because he is so full of consideration and constantly hesitates - fearing that the other might take a statement of his [Bohr's] point of view as an insufficient appreciation of the other's...' My Bohr is necessarily a little more coherent than this - and I have been told by various correspondents who knew him that in private, if not in public, he could be much more cogent and incisive than Schrödinger evidently found him.

The problem with Margrethe is that there is relatively little biographical material to go on. She and Niels were plainly mutually devoted, and everything suggests that she was as generally loved as he was. She had no scientific training, but Bohr constantly discussed his work with her, presumably avoiding technical language - though she must have become fairly familiar with even that since she typed out each draft of his papers. I suspect she was more gracious and reserved than she appears here, but she plainly had great firmness of character - in later life she was known as *Dronning* (Queen) Margrethe. She was always cooler about Heisenberg than Bohr was, and she was openly angry about his visit in 1941. According to Bohr she objected strongly to his being invited to the house, and relented only when Bohr promised to avoid politics and restrict the conversation to physics. Bohr himself always refused to be drawn about Heisenberg's trip in 1941, but she insisted, even after the war, even after all Heisenberg's attempts to explain, 'No matter what anyone says, that was a hostile visit.'

The problem with Heisenberg is his elusiveness and ambiguity, which is of course what the play is attempting to elucidate. The one thing about him that everyone agreed upon was what Max Born, his mentor in Göttingen, called 'his unbelievable quickness and precision of understanding.' The contrast with Bohr is almost comic. 'Probably [Bohr's] most characteristic property,' according to George Gamow, 'was the slowness of his thinking and comprehension.'

As a young man Heisenberg seems to have had an appealing eagerness and directness. Born described him as looking like a simple farm boy, with clear bright eyes, and a radiant expression on his face. Somebody else thought he looked 'like a bright carpenter's apprentice just returned from technical school.' Victor Weisskopf says that he made friends easily, and that everyone liked him. Bohr, after their first meeting in 1922, was delighted by Heisenberg's 'nice shy nature, his good temper, his eagerness and his enthusiasm.' There was something about him of the prize-winning student, who is good at everything required of him, and Bohr was not the only father-figure to whom he appealed. He had a somewhat similar relationship to Sommerfeld, his first professor in Munich, and in his difficulties with the Nazis he turned to two elders of German physics for counsel, Max Planck and Max von Laue. His closest friend and colleague was probably Carl Friedrich von Weizsäcker, who was younger than him, but it is strik-

ing that during his internment the person he chose to confide his explanation of the Hiroshima bomb to was not Weizsäcker, who was
interned with him (although he may well have discussed it with him
already), but the 66-year-old Otto Hahn.

The American physicist Jeremy Bernstein says that 'he had the
first truly quantum-mechanical mind - the ability to take the leap beyond the classical visualizing pictures into the abstract, all-but-
impossible-to-visualize world of the subatomic ...' Cassidy believes
that a great part of his genius was his 'ability to adopt a serviceable
solution regardless of accepted wisdom.' Rudolf Peierls stresses his
intuition. He would 'almost always intuitively know the answer to a
problem, then look for a mathematical solution to give it to him.' The
obverse of this, according to Peierls, is that 'he was always very cas-
ual about numbers' - a weakness that seems to have contributed to his
downfall - or his salvation - in the atomic bomb program.

Margrethe always found him difficult, closed, and oversensitive,
and this propensity to be withdrawn and inturned was exacerbated as
life went on - first by his political problems in the thirties, and then by
his efforts to reconcile the moral irreconcilables of his wartime work.
His autobiographical writing is rather stiff and formal, and his letters
to Bohr, even during the twenties and thirties, are correct rather than
intimate. Throughout the period of their closest friendship they addressed each other with the formal *Sie*, and switched to *du* only when
Heisenberg also had a chair.

The conversations that Heisenberg claimed such freedom to rec-
reate in his memoirs are stately. Much more plausibly colloquial is the
transcript of David Irving's long interview with him for *The Virus
House*, Irving's history of the German bomb program, though he is
still (naturally) watchful. In the transcripts of the relatively unguarded
conversations that the German atomic team had among themselves
during their internment, where Heisenberg emerges as the dominant
figure, both morally and practically, a certain hard-headed worldliness
can be detected. He is much concerned with professional prospects,
and with how they might make some money out of their wartime re-
searches. When one of the others says that if they agree to work on
atomic matters under Allied control they will be looked down upon as
traitors 'in the eyes of the masses,' Heisenberg replies: 'No. One must

do that cleverly. As far as the masses are concerned it will look as though we unfortunately have to continue our scientific work under the wicked Anglo-Saxon control, and that we can do nothing about it. We will have to appear to accept this control with fury and gnashing of teeth.'

There was always something a little sharp and harsh about him, something that at its best inspired respect rather than love, and that after the war occasioned really quite astonishing hostility and contempt. Even Samuel Goudsmit turned against him. Goudsmit was an old friend and colleague; when the investigators of the Alsos mission, the Allied agency for gathering intelligence on German atomic research, for which he was working, finally broke into Heisenberg's office in 1945, one of the first things they saw was a picture of the two of them together that Heisenberg had kept there as a memento of happier days. But when Goudsmit subsequently interrogated Heisenberg he found him arrogant and self-involved. Goudsmit had understandably bitter feelings at the time - he had just discovered the record of his parents' death in Auschwitz. Heisenberg was also caught in a false position. Confident that his team had been far ahead of the Americans, he offered Goudsmit his services in initiating them into the secrets of uranium fission. (Goudsmit did nothing to correct his misapprehension, which gave Heisenberg, when the truth finally came out, grounds for returning Goudsmit's bitterness.) In his superficial and strangely unimpressive book on Alsos, Goudsmit wrote about Heisenberg and his team with contemptuous dismissal, and in the year-long correspondence in the American press that followed its publication, accused him of self-importance and dishonesty.

Weisskopf gave a reception for Heisenberg during his trip to America in 1949, but about half the guests - including many people from the Los Alamos team - failed to appear, explaining to Weisskopf that they didn't want to shake the hand of the man who had tried to build a bomb for Hitler. Even Cassidy, who gives full measure to Heisenberg as a physicist in his biography, is notably cool and cautious in his assessment of Heisenberg's role in the German bomb program. Ronald Fraser, the British intelligence officer who escorted Heisenberg back to Copenhagen in 1947 (the British seem to have been frightened that he would defect to the Russians, or be kidnapped by them) replied to Irving's inquiry about the trip in tones of patronizing contempt that seem slightly unhinged. 'The whole story of "a kind of confrontation",' he wrote to Irving, 'in the matter of his 1941 natter with Bohr in the Tivoli Gardens [sic] is a typical Heisenberg fabrication - maybe a bit brighter than a thousand others, but like them all a product of his *Blut und Boden* guilt complex, which he rationalizes that quickly that the stories become *for him* the truth, the whole truth, and nothing but the truth. Pitiful, in a man of his mental stature.'

The historian Paul Lawrence Rose, who has focussed upon Heisenberg as an emblem for what he regards as the general failings of German culture, also takes a remarkably high moral tone. In a paper he wrote in 1984, entitled *Heisenberg, German Morality and the Atomic Bomb,* he talked about Heisenberg's 'guff,' his 'self-serving, self-deluding claims,' and his 'elementary moral stupidity.' After a further fourteen years research Professor Rose returned to the subject in 1998 in a full-length book which was published after the play was produced, and which has attracted considerable attention, *Heisenberg and the Nazi Atomic Bomb Project: a Study in German Culture*. His contempt for Heisenberg remains unmoderated. He believes that Heisenberg failed, in spite of his perfect readiness to serve the Nazi regime, because of his arrogance and wrong-headedness, and because he embodied various vices of German culture in general, and of the Nazi regime in particular, whose values he had absorbed.

It is a difficult book to read - Rose can scarcely quote a word of Heisenberg's without adding his own disparaging qualification. Here is a selection of his interjections on two facing pages taken more or less at random: '... self-incriminating ... a somewhat inadequate explanation ... this inconsistency ... the falseness of these lame excuses ... a characteristic Heisenberg lie ... Heisenberg's usual facile rationalizing ability ... Heisenberg then went on glibly to recollect ... the delusory nature of Heisenberg's memory ...'

You wonder at times whether it wouldn't look better if it were handwritten in green ink, with no paragraph breaks. Rose seems to be aware himself of the effect he is producing. He realizes, he says, that some readers may 'find distasteful the recurrent moral judgments passed on Heisenberg,' They may also, he thinks, be put off by what seems a 'lack of sympathy with German culture' - he cannot say, he confesses, that his 'British background' has made him entirely sympathetic to it. He is at pains to distance himself from any unfortunate echoes that this attitude may awaken: he hopes that readers will not accuse him of 'unthinkingly preaching a crude view of German "national character," whatever that term may mean.' What he is concerned with, he explains, is not that at all, but 'the enduring nature of what one might call the "deep culture" of Germany.... In this book I have tried to penetrate into how Germans think - or rather, perhaps, used to think - and to show how radically different are German and what I have termed "Western" mentalities and sensibilities.' It is this that underlies what he calls, without apparent irony, 'the Heisenberg problem.'

Some of his evidence induces a certain dizziness. He quotes without comment, as the epigraph to a chapter, a remark by Albert Speer, the Nazi Minister of Armaments: 'I do hope Heisenberg is not now claiming that they tried, for reasons of principle, to sabotage the project by asking for such minimal support!' It's true that any claim to have sabotaged the project, particularly for reasons of principle, would represent an astonishing departure from Heisenberg's habitual caution on the subject. But the question is not what Speer hoped, but whether Heisenberg *did* make such a claim.

So did he or didn't he? Rose doesn't tell us, and the only reference he gives is Gitta Sereny's new book, *Albert Speer: His Battle with Truth*. The allusion is to the crucial meeting at Harnack House in 1942, mentioned in the play. Speer said in his memoirs that he was 'rather put out' by the very small amount of money that Heisenberg requested to run the nuclear research program. In an earlier draft of the manuscript (the 'Spandau draft'), says Sereny, he had added in brackets the remark that Rose quotes - and Heisenberg, she says, 'did in fact try precisely that after the war.'

So he *did* make the claim! But when and where? Sereny doesn't tell us. The only references to the smallness of the sums of money he asked for that I can find in the record are the one quoted, by Speer himself, and another by Field Marshal Milch, Goering's deputy in the Luftwaffe, who was also present at the meeting. There's certainly nothing about it in Heisenberg's memoirs, or in Robert Jungk's book, *Brighter Than a Thousand Suns*, or in Heisenberg's long interview with Irving, or in the other two obvious places, his interview with *Der Spiegel* in 1967, when Irving's book was published, or his review of the book in the *Frankfurter Allgemeine Zeitung*. I hardly like to put myself forward to fill the gap, but so far as I know the only reference he made to the subject was posthumously and fictitiously in my play.

Sereny, like Rose, is markedly unenthusiastic about Heisenberg in general. She goes on to argue that Heisenberg's claims about his intentions in meeting Bohr in 1941 'are now shown by Speer's Spandau account to be false,' though quite how this is so she doesn't explain. About what she calls 'the facts' of the Copenhagen meeting she is remarkably brisk. In the conversation '... which Bohr subsequently reported to his associates at the Niels Bohr Institute, Heisenberg had made his political stand crystal clear. His team, he told Bohr, had gone some way towards discovering a way to produce an atom bomb. Germany was going to win the war, probably quite soon, and Bohr should join them now in their efforts.'

The idea that Heisenberg was inviting Bohr to work on the German bomb is on the face of it the least plausible out of all the possible interpretations that have been offered. It is completely at odds with what Weisskopf recalls Bohr as saying in 1948, and with what Bohr is on record as telling Chadwick at the time. In any case, the suggestion that Heisenberg thought he might be able to import someone half-Jewish into the most secret research program in Nazi Germany is frankly preposterous.

So what is Sereny's evidence for her account of the meeting? At this point the sense of vertigo returns, and one begins to have the feeling that one is in an Escher drawing, where the stairs up to the floor above somehow lead back to the floor one is already on, because the only reference she gives is ... Powers, Heisenberg's great champion, in *Heisenberg's War*.

And it's true - Powers *does* quote an opinion to this effect (and it's the only possible source for it anywhere, so far as I know). He says he was told by Weizsäcker that some person or persons unnamed in Copenhagen, 44 years after the event, had told *him* that this is what Bohr had said he had believed Heisenberg's intention to be. One might think that this is rather faint evidence. In any case, even if it really is what Bohr believed, it is of course not what Weizsäcker believed, or Powers either. They are reporting Bohr's alleged belief as a possible misapprehension on his part which might have explained his anger. Indeed, Powers's own reading of the situation is precisely the one that Sereny claims to be discredited by Speer's remark.

*

Goudsmit gradually modified his opinion, and his final judgment on Heisenberg, when he died in 1976, was a generous one which goes some way to expunging the dismissive tone of his book: 'Heisenberg was a very great physicist, a deep thinker, a fine human being, and also a courageous person. He was one of the greatest physicists of our time, but he suffered severely under the unwarranted attacks by fanatical colleagues. In my opinion he must be considered to have been in some respects a victim of the Nazi regime.'

Robert Jungk, one of the few authors who have ever attempted to defend Heisenberg, modified his opinion in the opposite direction. In *Brighter than a Thousand Suns*, originally published in 1956, he suggested that the German physicists had managed to avoid building nuclear weapons for conscientious reasons, and quoted Heisenberg as saying that, 'under a dictatorship active resistance can only be practiced by those who pretend to collaborate with the regime. Anyone speaking out openly against the system thereby indubitably deprives himself of any chance of active resistance.' But Jungk later changed his mind, and described the notion of passive resistance on the part of the German physicists as a 'myth'. He had contributed to spreading it, he said, out of an 'esteem for those impressive personalities which I have since realized to be out of place.'

For a really spirited and sustained defense Heisenberg had to wait until Powers published his book in 1993. It is a remarkable piece of work, journalistic in tone, but generous in its understanding and huge in its scope. A little too huge, perhaps, because Powers is unable to resist being side-tracked from the main narrative by the amazing byways that he perpetually finds opening off it. I recommend it particularly to other dramatists and screenwriters; there is material here for several more plays and films yet.

His central argument is that the Allied bomb program succeeded because of the uninhibited eagerness of the scientists to do it, particularly of those exiles who had known Nazism at first hand, and who were desperate to pre-empt Hitler; while the German program failed because of the underlying reluctance of scientists in Germany to arm Hitler with the bomb, however strong their patriotism, and however much they wanted to profit from the possibilities for research. 'Zeal was needed,' he says; 'its absence was lethal, like a poison that leaves no trace.'

But he goes further, and argues that Heisenberg 'did not simply withhold himself, stand aside, let the project die. He killed it.' He tries to show that at every point Heisenberg was careful to hold out enough hope to the authorities to ensure that he and his team were left in charge of the project, but never enough to attract the total commitment and huge investment that would have offered the only real hope of success. 'Heisenberg's caution saved him. He was free to do what he could to guide the German atomic research effort into a broom closet, where scientists tinkered until the war ended.'

Cassidy, reviewing the book in *Nature*, described it as a good story, but insisted that 'as history it is incredible.' Rose dismisses it as 'entirely bogus' and 'a scholarly disaster'. Powers acknowledged ruefully, in a recent letter to the *Times Literary Supplement*, that he had failed to convince any historian who had pronounced upon the matter.

The play is not an attempt to adjudicate between these differing views of Heisenberg's personality, or these differing accounts of his activities. But it would have been impossible to write it without taking *some* view of Powers' version of events, so here, for what it is worth, is a brief summary of the case, and of my own hesitant view of it. The evidence is confused and contradictory, and making any sense of it involves balancing probabilities and possibilities almost as indeterminable as Heisenberg found events inside the atom.

*

Some of the evidence undoubtedly appears to support Powers's thesis in its stronger form, that Heisenberg deliberately sabotaged the project.

In the first place there are two scraps of direct testimony. One is a message brought to America in 1941 by a departing German Jewish academic called Fritz Reiche. It was from Fritz Houtermans, the German physicist who had just realized that if they could get a reactor going it would produce plutonium, and that plutonium would be a fissile alternative to the U235 that they could not separate. Reiche testified later that he had passed it on to a group of scientists working at Princeton, including Wolfgang Pauli, John von Neumann, and Hans Bethe. As Rudolf Ladenburg, the physicist who arranged the meeting, recorded it afterwards, Houtermans wanted it to be known that 'a large number of German physicists are working intensively on the problem of the uranium bomb under the direction of Heisenberg,' and that 'Heisenberg himself tries to delay the work as much as possible, fearing the catastrophic results of a success.'

Rose dismisses Houtermans as a proven liar, and records that Reiche later appeared to withdraw his belief in Heisenberg's opposition to the project. But neither of these objections seems immediately relevant to the consistency of Reiche's and Ladenburg's testimony.

The second scrap of evidence is even more direct, but much more dubious. Heisenberg's American editor, Ruth Nanda Anshen, records receiving a letter from him in 1970 in which he claimed that, 'Dr Hahn, Dr von Laue and I falsified the mathematics in order to avoid the development of the atom bomb by German scientists.'

The letter itself has apparently vanished from the record. Rose nonetheless accepts it as beyond doubt genuine, and sees it as a yet more blatant attempt at self-justification. It is not, however, called into evidence by Powers, even though it would appear to support his case, and he mentions it only in his notes, and with the greatest reserve. Jeremy Bernstein, who seems to me the best-informed and most fair-minded of all Heisenberg's critics, and whose book *Hitler's Uranium Club* will be relied upon in understanding the scientific considerations that follow, dismisses it as 'incredible' and 'a chimera.' It is entirely at odds with Heisenberg's careful moderation in all his other references to the matter, and the inclusion of Hahn and von Laue in the plot is nonsensical. Hahn was a chemist, not a physicist, and, as will be plain from what comes later, had no knowledge whatsoever of the relevant mathematics, while von Laue is famous as an outspoken opponent of Nazism who never worked on the German nuclear program at all.

So much for the direct evidence, true or false. All the rest of the evidence is indirect, and relates to whether Heisenberg did actually have some understanding of the relevant physics and concealed it, or whether he failed out of ignorance. It centers on the question of critical mass, the amount of fissile material (U235 or plutonium) large enough to support an explosive chain reaction. An estimate of this amount was crucial to the decision about proceeding with a serious nuclear weapons program because of the enormous difficulty and expense of separating the U235 from the U238 that makes up the vast bulk of natural uranium, and the length of time it would take to develop a reactor capable of transmuting the uranium into plutonium. At the beginning of the war it was believed by scientists on both sides that the answer would be in tons, which put the possibility of producing it beyond practical consideration. The idea became imaginable only when two scientists working in Britain, Rudolf Peierls and Otto Frisch, did the calculation and realized quite how fast the reaction would go with fast neutrons in pure U235, and consequently how little fissile material you would need: not tons but kilograms. (The various ironies associated with this are explored in the play, and I will not repeat them here.)

Powers argues that the idea never became imaginable in Germany because Heisenberg 'cooked up a plausible method of estimating critical mass which gave an answer in tons.' He believes that Heisenberg 'well knew how to make a bomb with far less, but kept the knowledge to himself.'

There is a certain amount of evidence that the German team did at one point arrive at a much lower figure for the critical mass - indeed, for one in kilograms, that bore some relation to the estimate made by Frisch and Peierls, and to the actual mass of the Hiroshima bomb (56 kg). Manfred von Ardenne, who was running an alternative nuclear program for the German Post Office, later claimed in his memoirs that in the late autumn of 1941 he was informed independently by both Heisenberg and Hahn that they had worked out the criti cal mass for a U235 bomb and found it to be about 10 kilograms. This information was subsequently withdrawn by von Weizsäcker, who told him that he and Heisenberg had decided that a U235 bomb was impossible (because the heat of the reaction would expand the uranium too fast for it to continue). But Heisenberg, so far as I know, never commented on this, and von Weizsäcker, according to Bernstein, 'essentially denied' that any such conversation ever took place.

As Bernstein says, it is difficult to know what to make of all this - it is 'one of several brick walls anyone who studies this subject runs into.' I think it's difficult to take von Ardenne's recollection entirely literally. Hahn, as I noted before, plainly had no understanding of the mathematics, nor of any of the other issues involved, and, as we shall see, had to have them explained to him by Heisenberg later. On the other hand (and this story has more other hands than a Hindu god), in von Weizsäcker's report on the possibility of an American bomb program, written in September 1941, he talked about the destructive effects of a bomb weighing 5 kg. Then again, in February 1942 a brief progress report for German Army Ordance, authors unnamed, suggested without further explanation a critical mass of between 10 and 100 kg. And at the crucial meeting with Speer at Harnack House in June 1942, when Field Marshal Milch asked him how large an atomic bomb would have to be to destroy a city, Heisenberg replied, or so he said in his interview with Irving, that it, or at any rate its 'essentially active part,' would have to be 'about the size of a pineapple.'

In the end, though, I believe that the crucial piece of evidence lies elsewhere, in a source that was denied to everyone who wrote about Heisenberg until recently - the transcripts of the Farm Hall recordings. Bernstein, Powers, and Rose were the first commentators to have access to them.

Though of course they still don't reach the same conclusions from them.

*

The story of Farm Hall is another complete play in itself. Sir Charles Frank, the British atomic physicist, in his admirably fair and clear introduction to the text of the transcripts that was published in Britain, regrets that they were not released in time for Dürrenmatt to make use of.

At the end of the war troops of the Alsos mission, to which

Goudsmit was attached, made their way through what was left of the
German front line and located the remains of the German reactor at
Haigerloch, with the intention of finally reassuring themselves that
Germany would not be able to spring some terrible nuclear surprise at
the last moment. They also seized the team of scientists themselves,
making a special armed sortie to Urfeld, in Bavaria, to collect Heisenberg from his home. Hechingen, the nearby town where the team was
based, and Haigerloch itself were in the French sector. The scientists
were abstracted secretly, from under the noses of the French, and
brought back to Britain, where they were held, under wartime laws
and without anyone's knowledge, in a former Intelligence safe house -
Farm Hall, near Cambridge. The intention seems to have been partly
to prevent their passing on any atomic secrets to either of our other
two allies, the Russians and the French; partly to forestall any discussion of the possibility of nuclear weapons until we had completed and
used our own; and partly, perhaps, to save Heisenberg and the others
from the alternative solution to these problems proposed by one
American general, which was simply to shoot them out of hand.
     They were detained at Farm Hall for six months, during which
time they were treated not as prisoners but as guests. Hidden microphones, however, had been installed, and everything they said to each
other was secretly recorded. The existence of the transcripts from
these recordings was kept as secret as that of the prisoners. General
Groves, the head of the Allied bomb program, quoted from them in
his memoirs (1962), and Goudsmit plainly had access to them, which
he drew upon in his book on Alsos, but the British Government, perhaps to protect the feelings of the former detainees, some of them now
prominent in post-war German science, perhaps merely out of its
usual pathological addiction to secrecy, continued to block the release
of the papers themselves. Even Margaret Gowing was refused access
when she wrote her official history of British atomic policy in 1964,
and David Irving was refused again, in spite of strenuous efforts, for
The Virus House in 1967. The ban was maintained until 1992, when
the Government finally gave way to a combined appeal from leading
scientists and historians.
     The German originals are lost, and the translation was plainly
done under pressure, with little feeling for colloquial nuance, but the

transcripts are direct evidence of what Heisenberg and the others
thought when they were talking, as they believed, amongst themselves. The ten detainees represented a wide range of different attitudes. They ranged from Walther Gerlach, the Nazi Government's
administrator of nuclear research, and Kurt Diebner, who had been a
member of the Nazi party, to Max von Laue, who had been openly
hostile to the regime, who had never worked on the atomic program,
and whose inclusion in the party seems on the face of it mysterious.
Their conversations over the six month period reflect a similarly wide
range of attitudes and feelings. The general tone is pretty much what
one might expect from any group of academics deprived of their liberty
without explanation and cooped up together. There is, as one might
suppose, quite a lot of complaining, scheming, and mutual friction.

    One thing, though, seems to me to emerge quite clearly: for all
practical purposes German thinking had stopped at a reactor, and
there had been no eagerness at all to look beyond this to the possibility of weapons. Their shocked comments in the moment of unguarded
horror that followed the announcement of Hiroshima are particularly
revealing. The internees had been given the news by their (almost)
endlessly sympathetic and urbane gaoler-cum-host, Major Rittner, at
dinner-time, but Heisenberg had not believed it until he had heard it
with his own ears on the BBC nine o'clock news. 'They were completely stunned,' reported Rittner, 'when they realized that the news
was genuine. They were left alone on the assumption that they would
discuss the position ...'

    'I was absolutely convinced,' says Heisenberg, in the conversa-
tion that followed, 'of the possibility of our making an uranium engine [reactor] but I never thought that we would make a bomb and at
the bottom of my heart I was really glad that it was to be an engine
and not a bomb. I must admit that.' Weizsäcker says that he doesn't
think that they should make excuses now for failing, 'but we must
admit that we didn't want to succeed.' Gerlach: 'One cannot say in
front of an Englishman that we didn't try hard enough. They were our
enemies, although we sabotaged the war. There are some things that
one knows and one can discuss together but that one cannot discuss in
the presence of Englishmen.'

    In a letter written fourteen years later von Laue complained that, during their conversations at table in the following weeks, 'the version was developed that the German atomic physicists really had not wanted the atomic bomb, either because it was impossible to achieve it during the expected duration of the war or because they simply did not want to have it at all.' Von Laue's account of the elaboration of this sanitized 'version' (*Lesart* in German) has been seized upon by unsympathetic commentators, and contrasted with the encouraging prospects for atomic weapons that some of the physicists had undoubtedly held out to the Nazi authorities at various times during the earlier part of the war.

Well, we all reorganize our recollections, consciously or unconsciously, as time goes by, to fit our changed perceptions of a situation, and no doubt Heisenberg and his fellow-detainees did the same. But Bernstein locates the origins of the *Lesart* in those immediate reactions to the announcement of Hiroshima on the nine o'clock news. If this is so then I can only say that the team began to get their story together with quite remarkable spontaneity, speed, presence of mind, and common purpose. If they all thought as fast as this, and co-operated as closely, it's even more surprising that they didn't get further with the bomb.

To me, I have to say, those immediate and unprepared reactions suggest quite strongly that the first part of Powers's thesis, at any rate, is right, and that there *had* been the 'fatal lack of zeal' that he diagnosed. Perhaps Gerlach's claim, unchallenged by the others, that they had actually 'sabotaged the war' suggests at the very least a consciousness that quite a lot of stones had been left unturned.

*

But do the transcripts support Powers's contention that Heisenberg 'cooked up a plausible method of estimating critical mass which gave an answer in tons, and that he well knew how to make a bomb with far less, but kept the knowledge to himself'?

One preliminary point needs to be cleared out of the way first: the question whether Heisenberg understood an even more fundamental point, the difference between a reactor (which is operated by slow neutrons in natural uranium, or some other mixture of U238 and

U235) and a bomb (which functions with fast neutrons in pure U235 or plutonium). Goudsmit, who plainly had access to the transcripts when he wrote his book on Alsos, seems to have thought they supported his view that Heisenberg didn't. Before the transcripts were published Rose shared Goudsmit's dismissive view.

But, according to the transcripts, what Heisenberg tells Hahn that same night, when Gerlach has retired to sob in his room, and they are finally alone together, is that 'I always knew it could be done with 235 with fast neutrons. That's why 235 only [presumably = "only 235"] can be used as an explosive. One can never make an explosive with slow neutrons, not even with the heavy water machine [the German reactor], as then the neutrons only go with thermal speed, with the result that the reaction is so slow that the thing explodes sooner, before the reaction is complete.'

Bernstein (unlike Goudsmit) reads this and what follows as showing that Heisenberg *did* understand the difference between a reactor and a bomb, 'but that he did not understand either one very well - certainly not the bomb.' Rose now seems to accept that Heisenberg's remarks do indicate that he realized the bomb would have to be fissioned with fast neutrons (though he shows that in the past Heisenberg had been toying with the idea of some kind of vast exploding reactor).[1]

This same conversation between Heisenberg and Hahn, when they were alone together on that terrible night, seems to me also to resolve the question of Heisenberg's understanding of the critical mass beyond any reasonable doubt. He takes Hahn through what he believes to be the relevant calculation and tells him that the answer is 'about a ton.' I can't see any earthly reason why he should be rehearsing a fabricated calculation or a fabricated answer at this stage, in a private conversation with someone he seems to have trusted, after the German team are out of the race and in custody, and after someone

---

[1]Bernstein takes the trouble to explain in his book what few other commentators do — the difference between slow and fast neutrons: 'By definition, slow neutrons move with speeds of the order of a few kilometers a second, about the speeds that molecules at room temperature move in a gas. That is why these neutrons are also referred to as thermal. Fast neutrons, the kind that are emitted in many nuclear processes, move at speeds of tens of thousand of kilometers a second.'

else has in any case already built the bomb. If he had had the right calculation and the right answer up his sleeve all the time, now would surely have been the moment to produce them. I find it much more plausible that he was telling the simple truth when he said to Hahn just before this that 'quite honestly I have never worked it out as I never believed one could get pure 235.'

Earlier on in the evening, it's true, when everyone was present during the conversation immediately after the news bulletin, Hahn says to Heisenberg: 'But tell me why you used to tell me that one needed 50 kilograms of 235 in order to do anything.' (To which Heisenberg replies that he wouldn't like to commit himself for the moment.) This does seem to suggest that he *had* made a calculation of some sort earlier, as von Ardenne claimed - though it also surely destroys once and for all the improbable proposition that Hahn had been involved in it, or had made some kind of estimate of his own. Perhaps Heisenberg had made not so much a calculation as some kind of guess or estimate. Even if *was* a serious calculation, it seems most unlikely that it was the right calculation, or that it was one he had adhered to.

This is made clear to me (at last) by Jeremy Bernstein. I should explain that when I first read the Farm Hall transcripts, before I wrote the play, I was using the bare uncommented text published in Britain, unaware that there was also a completely different edition published in the US, incorporating Bernstein's detailed commentary. After the play was produced and published he was kind enough to send me it, and it illuminated a great many matters that I had not understood before. These are after all scientists talking to scientists, and they are reported verbatim with all the ellipses of spoken conversation, and with a further haze cast over the proceedings by translation. Bernstein is both a distinguished journalist and a professor of physics, and he has a long acquaintance with the history of atomic research. (He recalls being given the bare plutonium core of a bomb to hold on the Nevada test site in 1957; 'it was slightly warm to the touch, since plutonium is marginally radioactive.') He has a thorough understanding of the scientific issues involved, and is the ideal guide to the physics - though a slightly less percipient one, I think, to the psychology of the physicists

I'm pleased to discover for a start that he takes the same view of

Heisenberg's admission to Hahn about never having worked out the critical mass. He believes that it has to be taken at its face value, and he asks how it can be reconciled with the figure of 50 kg recalled by Hahn. He demonstrates that when Heisenberg attempts to do the calculation for Hahn he 'gets it wrong at every level' - he does the arithmetic wrong, and is in any case doing the wrong arithmetic. 'Knowing how scientists work,' says Bernstein, 'I find it implausible that he ever did the calculation correctly before. One can imagine even a Heisenberg forgetting a number - he was, in any case, not very good with numbers - but it is very difficult to imagine his forgetting a general method of calculation, a method that once led him to a more reasonable answer.'

The calculation of the critical mass is not the only thing that Heisenberg got wrong that night. Even when he revealed to Hahn that he understood how the critical mass could be reduced by the use of a reflective shield he suggested a material, carbon, that would have had the opposite effect to the one intended. Carbon is a good moderator for a reactor, and Heisenberg's proposing it for the 'tamper' in a bomb, says Bernstein, 'shows he was thinking like a reactor physicist, which, for the last two years, he was.'

These were of course Heisenberg's first thoughts off the top of his head in the wake of Hiroshima. A week later, with the help of what few details the newspapers had given of the two bombs, Heisenberg offered all his fellow-internees a lecture in which he presented a complete and considered account of how the Allies had done it. The inclusion in the lecture of quite fundamental matters, argues Powers, together with the questions which his hearers asked, make it clear that it was all news to everyone present except his closest associates. 'What the Farm Hall transcripts show unmistakably,' he says, 'is that Heisenberg did not explain basic bomb physics to the man in charge of the German bomb program [Gerlach] until after the war was over.' They 'offer strong evidence that Heisenberg never explained fast fission to Gerlach.' At the end of the lecture, says Powers, 'the German scientists, given a second chance, would have been ready to start building a bomb.'

Bernstein sees the lecture very differently. He demonstrates that Heisenberg's exposition is still marred by quite fundamental misconceptions. Heisenberg now seems to have 'the first inkling' of how to calculate the critical mass (though he still does the arithmetic wrong), but is not much nearer to the practicalities of building a bomb than his audience. What the novelty of a lot of this material suggests to Bernstein is simply that communications between the different sections of the German project were very poor.

As a nonscientist I can't offer any opinion on the physics. To my eyes, I have to say, Heisenberg does seem to have come a remarkably long way in a week - if, that is, he was starting more or less from scratch. And he surely must have been. It's really not plausible that he hadn't recollected more by this time if he actually had done the work. The conclusion seems to me inescapable: he hadn't done the calculation. If he had kept the fatal knowledge of how small the critical mass would be from anyone, as Powers argues, then it was from himself.

*

In the end, it seems to me, your judgment of Heisenberg comes down to what you make of his failure to attempt that fundamental calculation. Does it suggest incompetence or arrogance, as his detractors have claimed? It's possible. Even great scientists - and Bernstein agrees that Heisenberg was one of them - make mistakes, and fail to see possibilities that lesser men pick up; Heisenberg accepted that he had made a mistake in the formulation of uncertainty itself. And I think we have to accept Bernstein's judgment that, although he was the first person to be able to grasp the counter-intuitive abstraction of quantum mechanics, he was not so good at the practicalities of commonsense estimates and working arithmetic.

Or does the failure suggest something rather different? An unconscious reluctance to challenge the comforting and convenient assumption that the thing was not a practical possibility? Comforting and convenient, that is, if what he was trying to do was *not* to build a bomb. Is it all part of a general pattern of reluctance, as the first and more plausible part of Powers's thesis suggests? If so, you might wonder whether this reluctance was a state definite enough to be susceptible of explanation. Heisenberg was trapped in a seamless circle which explains itself: he didn't try the calculation because he didn't think it was worth doing - he didn't think it was worth doing because he didn't try it. The oddity, the phenomenon that requires explaining, is not this non-occurrence but its opposite - the escape of Frisch and Peierls from that same circle. It seems almost like a random quantum event; in which case, of course, it is no more explainable than its not happening.

After the war, certainly, Heisenberg was not just passively reluctant about any military application of nuclear power, but very actively so. In the 1950s, when there was a proposal to arm Federal Germany with nuclear weapons, he joined forces with Weizsäcker and others to fight a vigorous campaign that entirely and permanently defeated it.

There is also one small piece of evidence about his attitude during the war that Powers rather curiously doesn't comment on: the question of the cyclotron.

At the crucial meeting between Heisenberg and Speer in 1942, which seems finally to have scuppered all possibility of a German bomb, Heisenberg is reported to have emphasized the need to build a cyclotron. A cyclotron could have been used, as the cyclotrons in America were, for isotope separation, the great sticking-point in the German program. In the account of this meeting in his memoirs Speer says: 'Difficulties were compounded, Heisenberg explained, by the fact that Europe possessed only one cyclotron, and that of minimal capacity. Moreover, it was located in Paris and because of the need for secrecy could not be used to full advantage.' Powers mentions this, but does not go on to the obvious corollary: that if Speer's recollection is accurate, then Heisenberg was plainly lying, because he knew perfectly well that there was a second cyclotron to hand - at Bohr's institute in Copenhagen. This would suggest that his apparent anxiety to lay his hands on a machine that might actually separate some U235 was not quite what it seemed. Or, at the very least, that he placed Germany's war aims below his desire to protect Bohr's institute.

Perhaps Speer is simply wrong. It seems uncharacteristic of Heisenberg to have risked such a blatant falsehood, and he makes no mention of it in his own accounts of the meeting. All the same, when he went back to Copenhagen in 1944, after Bohr had fled, to adjudicate a German proposal to strip the institute of all its equipment, presumably

including the cyclotron, he seems to have contrived to leave it even
then still in Danish hands.

*

One of the forms of indeterminacy touched upon in the play is the
indeterminacy of human memory, or at any rate the indeterminability
of the historical record. There are various examples which I left out,
for fear of making the play even more tangled than it is. Some, such as
the difficulties about the amazingly realistic figure for the critical
mass that von Ardenne recollected being given by Heisenberg and
Hahn in 1941, I have already mentioned in this Postscript. There were
others. A minor one concerns whether there were two ships sent to
load the Jews of Copenhagen for deportation, as some witnesses recall, or a single one (named as the Wartheland). A more significant
point of dispute is the drawing which Heisenberg did or didn't make
for Bohr during their meeting in 1941.
        According to Hans Bethe, who was one of the team at Los Ala-
mos, Heisenberg drew a rough sketch to show Bohr the work that was
being done in Germany. Bohr evidently took it to Los Alamos with
him when he went, because Bethe (and others) recall it being passed
around at a meeting there. Bethe told Powers that Bohr believed it
represented a bomb; but the consensus of opinion at the meeting was
that it was a reactor. However, Aage Bohr, Niels's son, a physicist
himself (and another Nobel prizewinner), who was with his father in
Copenhagen during Heisenberg's visit, and with him again in Los
Alamos, was absolutely insistent that there was no drawing.
        If the story is true it might help to explain Goudsmit's insistence,
in the teeth of the evidence from Farm Hall, that Heisenberg couldn't
tell the difference between a reactor and a bomb. It would certainly
cast doubt on Heisenberg's recollection that the entire discussion with
Bohr in 1941 took place during the walk, and that Bohr broke off the
conversation almost as soon as it was broached. It seems improbable
to me that Heisenberg would have risked putting anything down on
paper, and if even so he had then I can't see why he didn't seize upon
it after the war, to support his claim that he had hinted to Bohr at the
German research on a bomb. I suppose it's possible that Bohr made

the sketch himself, to illustrate to his colleagues at Los Alamos what he thought Heisenberg was getting at, but the truth of the matter seems to be irretrievable.

*

I have had many helping hands with this play, both before it was produced in London and since. Sir John Maddox kindly read the text for me, and so did Professor Balázs L Gyorffy, Professor of Physics at Bristol University, who made a number of corrections and suggestions. I am also indebted to Finn Aaserud, the Director of the Niels Bohr Archive in Copenhagen, and to his colleagues there, for much help and encouragement. Many scientists and other specialists have written to me after seeing the play on the stage. They have mostly been extraordinarily generous and supportive, but some of them have put me right on details of the science, for which I am particularly grateful. They also pointed out two mathematical errors so egregious that the lines in question didn't make sense from one end to the other - even to me, when I re-read them. All these points have now been addressed, though I'm sure that other mistakes will emerge. So much new material has come to hand, in one way or another, that I have extensively overhauled and extended this Postscript to coincide with the production of the play in New York.

One matter of dispute that I have not been able to resolve completely concerns the part played by Max Born in the introduction of quantum mechanics. The matter was raised (with exemplary temperance) by his son, Gustav Born, who was concerned about the injustice he felt I had done to his father's memory. I was reluctant to make the play any more complex than it is, but I have since made adjustments both to the play itself and to this Postscript which go at any rate some way to meeting Professor Born's case. We are still at odds over one line, though, in which Heisenberg is said to have 'invented quantum mechanics.' I am quoting the judgment of other physicists here (including one not especially sympathetic to Heisenberg), but I realize that it is a huge over-simplification, and that it seems to compound the original injustice committed when Heisenberg was awarded the Nobel Prize in 1932 'for the creation of quantum mechanics,' while Born had to wait another 22 years to have his part acknowledged in the same way. The trouble is that I have not yet been able to think of another way of putting it briefly enough to work in spoken dialogue.

The American physicist Spencer Weart, in a letter to Finn Aaserud, very cogently pointed out that the calculation of the critical mass was much harder than I've made it seem for Heisenberg once Bohr has suggested it to him. 'Perrin failed to get it and his publication of a ton-size critical mass subtly misled everyone else, then Bohr and Wheeler failed, Kurchatov failed, Chadwick failed, all the other Germans and Russians and French and British and Americans missed it, even the greatest of them all for such problems, Fermi, tried but missed, everyone except Peierls.... Physics is hard.'

Some correspondents have objected to Heisenberg's line about the physicists who built the Allied bomb, 'Did a single one of them stop to think, even for one brief moment, about what they were doing?,' on the grounds that it is unjust to Leo Szilard. It's true that in March 1945 Szilard began a campaign to persuade the US Government not to use the bomb. A committee was set up - the Committee on Social and Political Implications - to allow the scientists working on the project to voice their feelings, and Szilard also circulated a petition among the scientists, 67 of whom signed it, which mentioned 'moral considerations,' though it did not specify what exactly these were.

But the main stated reasons for Szilard's second thoughts were not to do with the effects that the bomb would have on the Japanese - he was worried about the ones it would have on the Allies. He thought (presciently) that the actual use of the bomb on Japan would precipitate an atomic arms race between the United States and the Soviet Union. The Committee's report (which Szilard himself seems to have written) and the petition stressed the same points. By this time, in any case, the bomb was almost ready. It had been Szilard who urged the nuclear program in the first place, and at no point, so far as I know, while he worked for it (on plutonium production) did he ever suggest any hesitation about pursuing either the research or the actual manufacture of the bomb.

I think the line stands, in spite of Szilard's afterthoughts. The scientists had already presented their government with the bomb, and it is the question of whether the German scientists were ready or not to do likewise that is at issue in the play. If Heisenberg's team *had* built a bomb, I donut think they would have recovered very much moral credit by asking Hitler to be kind enough not to drop it on anyone - particularly if their objection had been the strain it might place upon post-war relations among the Axis powers.

*

One looming imponderable remains. *If* Heisenberg had made the calculation, and *if* the resulting reduction in the scale of the problem had somehow generated a real eagerness in both the Nazi authorities and the scientists, could the Germans have built a bomb? Frank believes that they could not have done it before the war in Europe was over - 'even the Americans, with substantial industrial and scientific advantage, and the important assistance from Britain and from ex-Germans in Britain did not achieve that (VE-Day, 8 May 1945, Trinity test, Alamogordo, 6 July 1945).' Speer (who as armaments minister would presumably have had to carry the program out) suggests in his memoirs that it might have been possible to do it by 1945, if the Germans had shelved all their other weapons projects, then two paragraphs later more cautiously changes his estimate to 1947; but of course he needs to justify his failure to pursue the possibility. Powers makes the point that, whatever the timetable was, its start date could have been much earlier. Atomic energy in Germany, he argues, attracted the interest of the authorities from the first day of the war. 'The United States, beginning in June 1942, took just over three years to do the job, and the Soviet Union succeeded in four. If a serious effort to develop a bomb had commenced in mid-1940, one might have been tested in 1943, well before the Allied bomber offensive had destroyed German industry.'

If this 'serious effort' had begun only after Heisenberg's visit to Copenhagen, as the play suggests might have happened if the conversation with Bohr had gone differently, then even this timetable wouldn't have produced a bomb until late 1944 - and by that time it was of course much less likely that German industry could have delivered. In any case, formidable difficulties remained to be overcome. The German team were hugely frustrated by their inability to find a successful technique for isolating U235 in any appreciable quantity, even though the experimental method, using Clusius-Dickel tubes, was of German origin. They could have tried one of the processes used successfully by the Allies, gaseous diffusion. This was another German invention, developed in Berlin by Gustav Hertz, but Hertz had lost his job because his uncle was Jewish. (It was, incidentally, the delays in getting the various American isotope-separation plants to function which meant that the Allied bomb was not ready in time for use against Germany.)

The failure to separate U235 also held up the reactor program, and therefore the prospect of producing plutonium, because they could not separate enough of it even for the purposes of enrichment (increasing the U235 content of natural uranium), so that it was harder to get the reactor to go critical. The construction of the reactor was further delayed because Walther Bothe's team at Heidelberg estimated the neutron absorption rates of graphite wrongly, which obliged the designers to use heavy water as a moderator instead. The only source of heavy water was a plant in Norway, which was forced to close after a series of attacks by Norwegian parachutists attached to Special Operations Executive, American bombers, and the Norwegian Resistance. Though perhaps, if a crash program had been instituted from the first day of the war, enough heavy water might have been accumulated before the attacks were mounted.

If, if, if.... The line of ifs is a long one. It remains just possible, though. The effects of real enthusiasm and real determination are incalculable. In the realm of the just possible they are sometimes decisive.

*

Anyone interested enough in any of these questions to want to sidestep the fiction and look at the historical record should certainly begin with:

Thomas Powers: *Heisenberg's War* (Knopf 1993; Cape 1993)

David Cassidy: *Uncertainty: The Life and Science of Werner Heisenberg* (W H Freeman 1992)

Abraham Pais: *Niels Bohr's Times* (OUP 1991) - Pais is a fellow nuclear physicist, who knew Bohr personally, and this, in its highly ec-
centric way, is a classic of biography, even though Pais has not much
more sense of narrative than I have of physics, and the book is organized more like a scientific report than the story of someone's life. But
then Bohr notoriously had no sense of narrative, either. One of the
tasks his assistants had was to take him to the cinema and to explain
the plot to him afterwards.

Werner Heisenberg: *Physics and Beyond* (Harper & Row 1971) - In
German, *Der Teil und das Ganze*. His memoirs.

Jeremy Bernstein: *Hitler's Uranium Club, the Secret Recordings at
Farm Hall*, introduced by David Cassidy (American Institute of Physics, Woodbury, New York 1996)

or the British edition of the transcripts:

Operation Epsilon, the Farm Hall Transcripts, introduced by Sir
Charles Frank. (Institute of Physics Publishing 1993)

Also relevant:

Heisenberg: *Physics and Philosophy*. (Penguin 1958)

Niels Bohr: *The Philosophical Writings of Niels Bohr* (Oxbow Press,
Connecticut 1987)

Elizabeth Heisenberg: *Inner Exile* (Birkhauser 1984) - In German *Das
politische Leben eines Unpolitischen*. Defensive in tone, but revealing
about the kind of anguish her husband tended to conceal from the
world; and the source for Heisenberg's ride home in 1945.

David Irving: *The German Atomic Bomb* (Simon & Schuster 1968) -
in UK as *The Virus House* (Collins 1967). The story of the German
bomb program.

Paul Lawrence Rose: *Heisenberg and the Nazi Atomic Bomb Project*
(U of California Press 1998)

Records and Documents Relating to the Third Reich, II German

112   COPENHAGEN

Atomic Research, Microfilms DJ29-32. (EP Microform Ltd, Wakefield) Irving's research materials for the book, including long verbatim interviews with Heisenberg and others. The only consultable copy I could track down was in the library of the Ministry of Defence, London

Archive for the History of Quantum Physics, microfilm. Includes the complete correspondence of Heisenberg and Bohr. A copy is available for reference in the Science Museum Library, London. Bohr's side of the correspondence is almost entirely in Danish, Heisenberg's in German apart from one letter.

Leni Yahil: *The Rescue of Danish Jewry*, (Jewish Publication Society of America, Philadelphia 1969)

There are also many interesting sidelights on life at the Bohr Institute in its golden years in:

French & Kennedy, eds: *Niels Bohr, A Centenary Volume* (Harvard 1985)

and in the memoirs of Hendrik Casimir, George Gamow, Otto Frisch, Otto Hahn, Rudolf Peierls, and Victor Weisskopf.

For the subsequent challenges to the Copenhagen Interpretation:

David Deutsch: *The Fabric of Reality* (Allen Lane 1997)

Murray Gell-Mann: *The Quark and the Jaguar* (W H Freeman 1994; Little, Brown 1994)

Roger Penrose: *The Emperor's New Mind* (OUP 1989)

The actual 'two-slits' experiment was carried out by Dürr, Nonn, and Rempe at the University of Konstanz, and is reported in *Nature* (3 September 1998). There is an accessible introduction to the work in the same issue by Peter Knight, and another account of it by Mark Buchanan (boldly entitled 'An end to uncertainty') in *New Scientist* (6 March 1999).

POST-POSTSCRIPT

I made a number of changes to the text of the play, as I have explained above, in response to suggestions and criticisms I received during the run of the play in London, and to new material I came across. The production in New York, however, opened up a much broader and more fundamental debate. A number of commentators expressed misgivings about the whole enterprise. Paul Lawrence Rose, the most outspoken of the play's critics, even managed to detect in it a 'subtle revisionism ... more destructive than Irving's self-evidently ridiculous assertions - more destructive of the integrity of art, of science, and of history.'

One of the most frequent complaints about the play in America was that I should have laid more stress on the evils of the Nazi regime, and in particular upon the Holocaust; it was pointed out that Heisenberg's visit to Copenhagen in 1941 coincided with the Wannsee Conference. It was argued that I should have put the visit in the context of a number of subsequent trips he made during the course of the war to other occupied countries. It was also felt that I should have laid more stress than I did on Heisenberg's stated view that Germany's conquests, at any rate in Eastern Europe, were justified, and that her victory over Russia was to be welcomed.

With hindsight I think I accept some of these criticisms. I should perhaps have had Heisenberg justify Germany's war aims on the Eastern front direct, instead of having Bohr refer to his arguments in one angry but passing aside. I should perhaps have found some way to make the parallel with all the other trips that were found offensive, and about whose purpose there was none of the mystery which had seemed to attach to the one to Copenhagen.

About a greater stress on the evil of the Nazi regime I'm not so sure. I thought that this was too well understood to need pointing out. It is after all the *given* of the play; this was precisely why there was (or should have been) a problem facing Heisenberg, and us in understanding him. In any case the play returns to the persecution of Jews in Nazi Germany again and again, from the suppression of so-called 'Jewish physics' (relativity) to the enforced flight of all the Jewish physicists, the death of Goudsmit's parents in Auschwitz, and the attempt by the SS to deport the Jewish population of Denmark to the death camps, which Margrethe Bohr describes as 'that great darkness inside the human soul ... flooding out to engulf us all.'

Some of the criticisms were even more radical. The play turns on the difficulty of determining why Heisenberg made his trip. For a number of commentators there was no problem at all - they knew the correct explanation for certain; though what that explanation was varied from one to another. For some it was Heisenberg's desire to persuade Bohr of the rightness of Germany's war aims and of its inevitable victory; for Rose and others he was on a spying mission, to find out through Bohr if the Allies were also working on an atomic bomb.

I agree that Heisenberg may have wished to present the German case to Bohr; but he surely didn't go all the way to Copenhagen *just* to do that. I also agree about the spying. But then so does my Heisenberg. He tells Bohr that he wanted 'some hint, some clue' about whether there was an Allied nuclear program. This seems to me to be commonsense; he would have had to be insanely incurious not to seize any chance he could to find out whether the Allies might drop atomic bombs on his country. There is surely no contradiction at all with what he himself claimed his purpose was - to discuss whether the German team were justified in working on a German weapon. Any information he could get about the other side's intentions would have been a prerequisite for deciding what to do.

Some criticisms I reject, and I should like to put the record straight. Professor Rose suggested that I had 'fantasized' Heisenberg's fear that he was in danger of his life from the Gestapo for talking to Bohr. Not so - I was simply expanding upon what the real Heisenberg said. Jonothan Logan, a physicist writing in *American Scientist*, dismissed as misleading the fictitious Bohr's assertion that in June 1942 Heisenberg had been slightly ahead of Fermi in Chicago. The context makes plain that this was in terms of neuron multiplication, and the claim was based on what David Cassidy says in his biography of Heisenberg. The correctness of Cassidy's assessment was verified for me, after much inquiry on my part, by Al Wattenberg, one of the editors of Fermi's *Collected Papers*.

All these are at any rate debatable points. Other criticisms I found extremely difficult to make sense of - some even to credit. Professor Rose, who detected the subtle revisionism of the play, found a particularly sinister significance in one detail - the fictitious Heisenberg's remarking upon the neatness of the historical irony whereby the crucial calculation (of the critical mass), which persuaded the Allies of the possibility of building a nuclear weapon, was made by a German and an Austrian, driven into exile in Britain because they were Jewish. Professor Rose saw this as an attempt to blame 'the Jews' for the bomb's invention.

A little more extraordinary still was the view of the play taken by Gerald Holton, Professor of Physics and Professor of the History of Science Emeritus at Harvard. He saw it as being 'structured in good part' to reflect the thesis advanced by Powers, that Heisenberg had correctly calculated the critical mass but concealed it by 'cooking up' a false result. By the time the play was produced in New York, he believed, I had been forced (by Bernstein) to lay this idea aside, so that I now had an 'unsolvable problem' with the motivation of the play.

I can only suppose that Professor Holton was misled because in the Postscript I speak warmly and gratefully about Powers' book. It has been much attacked, but I continue to admire the generosity of its tone, and the range of Powers' research. I also agree with the first part of his thesis (lack of zeal). But then so does Holton himself, and so, he says, does everyone else who has studied the matter. In the Postscript, however, I make abundantly clear that I don't accept Powers' view about the 'cooking up' and never did.

But you don't even need to read the Postscript to discover this, because it's all over the play itself. The central argument turns on Heisenberg's confession to Otto Hahn that he had *not* attempted the calculation. By my count there are something like thirty-five speeches devoted to establishing this, to asking why he hadn't attempted it, and to suggesting what might have happened if he had. How anyone could give the play even the most cursory glance and fail to notice this is difficult to understand.

Even harder to credit was the reaction in some quarters to the 'strange new quantum ethics' proposed by the fictitious Heisenberg. I suppose I should have erected a flashing 'IRONY' sign in front of it. This allusion is to his insight, in his original introduction of quantum mechanics, that physics should be limited to the measurement of what we could actually observe - the external effects of events inside the atom. We should need a similar kind of ethics, he suggests in my play, if we judged people purely on the external effects of their actions, without regard to their intentions. According to Professor Holton, Heisenberg 'exults' that under the new dispensation there would be a place in heaven even for him. Professor Holton fails to mention that Heisenberg also 'exults' that, under the new quantum ethical rules, there would also be a place in heaven for the SS man who seemed ready to murder him in 1945, simply because in the end he settled for a pack of American cigarettes instead. Jonothan Logan manages to believe that I am seriously proposing even the SS man's assumption into heaven.

Let me make it absolutely unambiguous: my Heisenberg is saying that we *do* have to make assessments of intention in judging actions. (The epistemology of intention is what the play is about!) He is saying that Bohr will continue to inspire respect and love, in spite of his involvement in the building of the Hiroshima and Nagasaki bombs; and that he himself will continue to be regarded with distrust in spite of his failure to kill anyone. The reaction of Holton, Rose, and others to the play is perhaps an oblique testimony to the truth of this judgment.

*

One of the most striking comments on the play was made by Jochen Heisenberg, Werner Heisenberg's son, when I met him, to my considerable alarm, after the premiere of the play in New York. 'Of course, your Heisenberg is nothing like my father,' he told me. 'I never saw my father express emotion about anything except music. But I understand that the characters in a play have to be rather more forthcoming than that.'

This seems to me a chastening reminder of the difficulties of representing a real person in fiction, but a profoundly sensible indication of the purpose of attempting it, which is surely to make explicit the ideas and feelings that never quite get expressed in the confusing onrush of life, and to bring out the underlying structure of events. I take it that the nineteenth-century German playwright Friedrich Hebbel was making a similar point when he uttered his great dictum (one that every playwright ought to have in pokerwork over his desk): 'In a good play everyone is right.' I assume he means by this not that the audience is invited to approve of everyone's actions, but that everyone should be allowed the freedom and eloquence to make the most convincing case that he can for himself. Whether or not this is a universal rule of playwriting it must surely apply to this particular play, where a central argument is about our inability, in our observation of both the physical world and the mental, ever to escape from particular viewpoints.

I suppose this is what sticks in some people's throat - that my Heisenberg is allowed to make a case for himself - even to criticize others. His claims about his intentions are strongly contested by another character in the play, Margrethe Bohr. Neither Heisenberg nor Margrethe Bohr, so far as I can see, is presented as winning the argument. I don't see why my Margrethe shouldn't be allowed to express her suspicions of Heisenberg much more sharply and woundingly than the real Margrethe's habitual courtesy would ever have permitted, and I don't see why my Heisenberg shouldn't be free to express the deeper feelings that the real Heisenberg remained silent about. Why shouldn't he have the same conflicting loyalties and the same mixed motives and emotions that we all have? Why shouldn't he try to juggle principle and expediency, as we all do? Why shouldn't he fear his country's defeat, and its destruction by nuclear weapons? Why shouldn't he lament its ruin and the slaughter of its citizens?

I can imagine it being asked how far I think this principle should be carried. Do I believe that a fictitious Hitler should be accorded the same privileges? I can see all the problems of exhibiting Hitler on the stage, but I can't see any point in attempting it at all if he is to be simply an effigy for ritual humiliation. Why should we be asked to endure a representation of his presence if he doesn't offer us some understanding of what was going on inside his head from his own point of view? The audience can surely be trusted to draw its own moral conclusions.

*

The most surprising result of the debate set off by the production of the play, though, has been the release of the Bohr documents.

I was told privately about the existence of at any rate one of the documents at a symposium on the play organized in Copenhagen by the Niels Bohr Archive in the autumn of 1999. Heisenberg had made public his own version of the 1941 meeting with Bohr, chiefly in two places: a memorandum written in 1957 to Robert Jungk, who was preparing the material for *Brighter Than a Thousand Suns*, and his memoirs, published in 1969. Bohr, however, had never publicly given his side of the story, and historians had been obliged to rely upon what other people (chiefly his son Aage - also a physicist, and later a Nobel prizewinner himself - and his colleague Stefan Rozental) recalled him as saying about it.

In 1957, however, Bohr had apparently been so angered by Heisenberg's version, when he read it in Jungk's book, that he had written to Heisenberg dissenting, and giving his own account. He had never sent the letter, though, and at his death in 1962 it had been placed in the Archive by his family, not to be released for another fifty years. This was all my informant was prepared to tell me.

I said nothing about this because I believed that I had been told in confidence. The existence of the letter was first publicly mentioned, as far as I know, by Professor Holton, at a further symposium on the play organized in New York in March 2000 on the occasion of its production there. He said that he had actually seen the letter - he had been shown it by the Bohr family. He felt bound not to divulge its contents, but I recall him as promising that when it was finally made public, in 2012, it would entirely change our view of the meeting.

Now that cat was out of the bag, and at yet another symposium on the play, at the Niels Bohr Archive in September 2001, it was announced that the Bohr family had decided to release the letter early. It also turned out that there was not just the one letter but various alternative drafts and notes relating to it. When they were finally published on the web in February 2002 the whole question of the visit was accorded even wider attention in the press that ever before.

The documents seem to me to bear out remarkably well the very detailed reconstruction made of Bohr's attitude by Powers from other sources. The most surprising thing to me in Bohr's first attempt at the letter is its remarkably sharp tone - particularly coming from a man so celebrated for his conciliatoriness:

> I think that I owe it to you to tell you that I am greatly amazed to see how much your memory has deceived you ....
>
> Personally, I remember every word of our conversations, which took place on a background of extreme sorrow and tension for us here in Denmark. In particular, it made a strong impression both on Margrethe and me, and on everyone at the Institute that the two of you spoke to, that you and Weizsäcker expressed your definite conviction that Germany would win and that it was therefore quite foolish for us to maintain the hope of a different outcome of the war and to be reticent as regards all German offers of cooperation. I also remember quite clearly our conversation in my room at the Institute, where in vague terms you spoke in a manner that could only give me the firm impression that, under your leadership, everything was being done in Germany to develop atomic weapons and that you said that there was no need to talk about details since you were completely familiar with them and had spent the past two years working more or less exclusively on such preparations. I listened to this without speaking since [a] great matter for mankind was at issue in which, despite our personal friendship, we had to be regarded as representatives of two sides engaged in mortal combat.

It is a revelation to have all this in Bohr's own voice, and I wish it had been available when I wrote the play. I recognize that the real Bohr remained much angrier for much longer than my character, that he claimed to have paid much closer attention to what Heisenberg said, and that he claimed to recall it much more clearly.

Does it really modify our view of what Heisenberg said, though, and of what his intentions were?

Slightly, I think, but not fundamentally. There has never been any disagreement, for a start, that Heisenberg publicly told various people at the Institute that Germany was going to win the war, and that her aims, at any rate in the E:.st, were justified. Then again, Aage and Rozental were both already on record as recalling Bohr's saying that Heisenberg had talked about the military applications of atomic energy. According to Aage: 'My father was very reticent and expressed his skepticism because of the great technical difficulties that had to be overcome, but he had the impression that Heisenberg thought that the new possibilities could decide the outcome of the war if the war dragged on.' According to Rozental: 'I can only remember how excited Bohr was after that conversation and that he quoted Heisenberg for having said something like, "You must understand that if I am taking part in the project then it is in the firm belief that it can be done."'

The letter, however, is the first direct confirmation that Bohr believed he was being urged to accept German 'offers of cooperation,' which is what Weizsäcker suspected he may have understood Heisenberg to be suggesting. It's not clear from the letter what Bohr thought this 'cooperation' would entail, and the recollection may not be entirely at odds with what Weizsäcker recalls Heisenberg as telling Bohr - that he ought to establish contact with the staff of the German Embassy for his own safety.

Some of the differences between Bohr's account of the meeting and Heisenberg's are less clear-cut than Bohr's indignation makes them appear. According to Heisenberg, in his memorandum to Jungk, he told Bohr he knew that the use of uranium fission for making weapons was 'in principle possible, but it would require a terrific technical effort, which one can only hope cannot be realized in this war.' Bohr, he said, was shocked, 'obviously assuming that I had intended to convey to him that Germany had made great progress in the direction of manufacturing atomic weapons.' This is not all that different in substance, it seems to me, from what Bohr recalls.

The same is true when Bohr goes on to dispute Heisenberg's interpretation of his reaction:

That my silence and gravity, as you write in the letter,

could be taken as an expression of shock at your reports that it was possible to make an atomic bomb is a quite peculiar misunderstanding, which must be due to the great tension in your own mind. From the day three years earlier when I realized that slow neutrons could only cause fission in uranium 235 and not 238, it was of course obvious to me that a bomb with certain effect could be produced by separating the uraniums.... If anything in my behavior could be interpreted as shock, it did not derive from such reports but rather from the news, as I had to understand it, that Germany was participating vigorously in a race to be the first with atomic weapons.

The difference between the 'shock' that Heisenberg diagnosed and the more dignified 'silence and gravity' that Bohr himself recalled dissolves a little in a later draft of the letter, where Bohr refers to his reaction as 'alarm.' His assertion that he already understood about the possibility of producing a weapon based on fission is moreover a simplification which is not quite supported by his subsequent behavior. He had in fact up to that moment believed that it was a practical impossibility, because of the difficulty of separating the fissile U-235, and Heisenberg could not tell him why the balance of probability had now changed - because of the German team's realization that a reactor, if they could get one going, would produce plutonium as an alternative. After Heisenberg's visit, according to Rozental, he was sufficiently shaken by Heisenberg's confidence to go back to the blackboard and rework all his calculations. Even so he seems to have remained unconvinced when he got his guarded report on the meeting through to Chadwick, his contact with British intelligence, and said: 'Above all I have to the best of my judgment convinced myself that in spite of all future prospects any immediate use of the latest marvelous discoveries of atomic physics is impracticable.'

The real kernel of the apparent disagreement about the meeting emerges only in later drafts of the letter, where Bohr says that 'there was no hint on your part that efforts were being made by German physicists to prevent such an application of atomic science.' This appears to be a rebuttal of some claim make by Heisenberg. The belief that Heisenberg made some such claim seems to be widespread. Professor Holton suggests that my play is 'based in large part on Heisenberg's published claim that for him an impeding moral compunction may have existed about working on atomic energy.'

But nowhere, so far as I know, did Heisenberg ever make the claim that Bohr seems to have attributed to him. There is no mention of it in the memorandum to Jungk. Even in the expanded account of the meeting that he gave in his memoirs he remained extremely cautious: 'I hinted that ... physicists ought perhaps to ask themselves whether they should work in this field at all.... An enormous technical effort was needed. Now this, to me, was so important precisely because it gave physicists the possibility of deciding whether or not the construction of atom bombs should be attempted. They could either advise their governments that atom bombs would come too late for use in the present war, and that work on them therefore detracted from the war effort, or else contend that, with the utmost exertions, it might just be possible to bring them into the conflict. Both views could be put forward with equal conviction....'

One might think this sounds a quite implausibly judicious rendering of anything he might have said. The fact remains, however, that he is not claiming to have made any efforts to prevent work on weapons. He is not even claiming that up to this point the German team had exercised the option of offering discouraging advice, only that they might at some point if they so chose. In any case, Heisenberg says that Bohr 'was so horrified by the very possibility of producing atomic weapons that he did not follow the rest of my remarks.'

Some reports on the release of the documents have suggested that they refute a claim made by Heisenberg to have offered Bohr a 'deal,' whereby the German physicists would discourage their government from proceeding with nuclear weapons if Allied physicists would do likewise. I suppose the implication of Heisenberg's indeterminate phrase 'the physicists' is that this applied to the physicists on both sides, but the only evidence I can find for Heisenberg having made any more definite suggestion than this is in a part of the memorandum to Jungk which is quoted by Powers: 'I then asked Bohr once again if, because of the obvious moral concerns, it would be possible for all physicists to agree among themselves that one should not even attempt work on atomic bombs....' This might perhaps be interpreted as a tentative hint at some possible arrangement, though in the interview he gave to David Irving for *The Virus House* in 1965 he seems to be retreating even from this, and says merely that Bohr 'perhaps sensed that I should prefer it if physicists in the whole world would say: We will not make atom bombs.' The remark to Jungk was not quoted by him in his book, and so presumably was not seen by Bohr in 1957. In his letter, in any case, Bohr makes no reference to any such claim, or to having understood any such offer at the time.

There are discrepancies in every other aspect of the evidence relating to this meeting, and it is scarcely surprising that there are some to be found between the two participants' own accounts. In both cases they are attempting to recollect something that happened sixteen years earlier, and their perceptions are inevitably colored by strong feelings and conflicting loyalties. On the whole, I think, it's surprising how slight the differences of substance are, and how readily most of them can be understood in the circumstances.

The most remarkable point of agreement, it seems to me now that I have had time to reflect upon it, was missed by everyone who wrote about the letters at the time of their release, myself included: Bohr's confirmation of Heisenberg's claim to have overridden all normal obligations of secrecy. Heisenberg did indicate to him, he agrees, that there was a German atomic program; that he himself was involved in it; and that he now believed it in principle possible to build atomic weapons.

Whatever Heisenberg was officially licensed or ordered to do in Copenhagen, I cannot believe that it included revealing the existence of one of the most secret research programs in Germany - least of all to an enemy alien who was known to be in contact with Allied scientists (Bohr was at this point still contributing to the U.S. journal *The Physical Review*), and also to be under observation because of his hostile attitude to Nazism and his extensive help for its victims. Heisenberg must have done this on his own initiative, and he must have been aware that Bohr would pass the information on, if he possibly could, to his contacts in Britain or the U.S. This, it seems to me, goes a considerable way to supporting the account that Heisenberg subsequently gave of his intentions.

*

The only really clear-cut disagreement between the two accounts is about a circumstantial detail - where the meeting took place. Bohr talks about 'our conversation in my room at the Institute.' Heisenberg, on the other hand, recalls in his memoirs visiting the Bohrs' home in Carlsberg, and finally broaching 'the dangerous subject' on their evening walk. This version is reinforced by what he recalls of his attempt to reconstruct with Bohr the 1941 meeting when he returned to Copenhagen in 1947. He was convinced, he said, that the conversation had taken place during 'a nocturnal walk on Pile Allé, which is very close to Carlsberg, and four kilometers away from the Institute. (Bohr at the time, according to Heisenberg, thought it had been in his study - but in his study at home in Carlsberg.)

Bohr himself lends some color to the Carlsberg version by remarking in the letter that 'every word of our conversations ... made a strong impression both on Margrethe and me.' It seems highly unlikely that Margrethe would have been present at any of the various meetings in the Institute; I don't think that any of the other participants mention her. Jochen Heisenberg recalls his father showing him the street where he said he had walked with Niels Bohr in 1941, though he can't now remember the name of it, only that it was tree-lined (which Pile Allé is).

There is a secondhand account of the meeting given to Thomas Powers by Ruth Nanda Anshen, Heisenberg's American editor, who said that she was told it by Bohr, and that his assistant Aage Petersen confirmed it. According to Powers, in *Heisenberg's War*, Bohr told Anshen that 'the invitation had cost him much agony - he wanted to sit down to dinner with Heisenberg, but his wife, Margrethe, objected, and Bohr couldn't make up his mind what to do. Finally his assistant Aage Peterson suggested that Bohr should write down his objections to Heisenberg's visit, then read them carefully a day or two later, and decide. This Bohr did; the old friendship seemed to him stronger than

the objections, and he told his New York friend that he finally obtained Margrethe's agreement with a solemn promise to discuss only
physics with Heisenberg - not politics.'

On the other hand Abraham Pais, Bohr's biographer, after making inquiries among Bohr's surviving colleagues just before his own
death in 2000, concluded that Heisenberg had never been to the
Bohrs' home. Even Heisenberg's own testimony is not entirely con-
sistent. According to his biographer, David Cassidy, he made an earlier statement in which he 'remembered that his most important talk
with Bohr occurred one evening as they strolled along a tree-lined
path in the large and secluded Faelledpark, just behind Bohr's institute.' Weizsäcker, who recalled that he met Heisenberg only ten minutes after the meeting with Bohr was over (the two men had parted
company, he said, 'in a friendly way,' but Heisenberg had immediately told him: 'I'm afraid it's gone completely wrong') agreed that it
had taken place in the open air, but introduced another location altogether - Langlinie, the raised walk beside the harbor, miles from either Carlsberg or the Institute.

*

Some light on this question has now been cast, nine months after
the release of the Bohr documents, by the emergence of yet another
letter. This one was written by Heisenberg, and revealed by Dr.
Helmut Rechenberg, the director of the Werner Heisenberg Archive in
Göttingen[2]. The Heisenberg family, who released it, seem not to have
taken in its implications earlier.

It makes no direct reference to the disputed conversation itself,
but is a much more reliable guide to the circumstances surrounding it
than the accounts we have had so far, because it was written not sixteen years after the event but during the week that Heisenberg was
actually there. In fact it's in three sections, dated respectively to three
different evenings - Tuesday (September 16, the day after he arrived),
Thursday, and Saturday - and it was posted to his family in Leipzig as

---

[2]In a Heisenberg Centenary Festschrift issued by the Sächsische Akademie
der Wissenschaften. The letter will be published in 2003 in a collection of his
correspondence edited by his daughter Maria Hirsch.

soon as he got back to Berlin.

It clears up one small point of dispute completely. Heisenberg *did* go to the house - and more than once. He also records various visits to the Institute, and the sheer number and variety of meetings that the two men had during the week supports the claim that Heisenberg's chief reason for making the trip was to see Bohr. The conflation of the different occasions in the participants' memories also probably explains some of the later discrepancies.

The first visit to the Bohrs was late on the Monday evening, as soon as Heisenberg had got off the train from Berlin. The sky, he recorded, was clear and starry, but in the Bohrs' house he found rather darker weather. 'The conversation swiftly turned to the human questions and misfortunes of our time; about the human ones there was spontaneous agreement; on the political question I found it difficult to cope with the fact that even in a man like Bohr thoughts, feelings, and hatred cannot be completely separated.'

It's just possible that the fateful conversation occurred at this first meeting, either in the house - where, said Heisenberg, 'later I sat for a long time alone with Bohr' - or later still, after midnight, when Bohr saw him to the tram. But they were accompanied to the tram stop by Hans, one of Bohr's sons, who would surely have remembered it and remarked upon it if it had happened then. And if Weizsäcker's recollection is even remotely accurate then the conversation can't have occurred at any point during this first meeting, because he himself arrived in Copenhagen only on the Wednesday.

The most likely occasion was two days later, during Heisenberg's second visit, on the Wednesday evening. (This time there was a young Englishwoman present, who 'decently withdrew' during 'the unavoidable political conversations, in which the role of defending our system of course automatically fell upon me.') Dr. Rechenberg suggests plausibly that Bohr accompanied Heisenberg alone part of the way back to his hotel, where Weizsäcker was waiting for him.

The real surprise of the letters, though, is that Heisenberg was invited back to the Bohrs' home for a *third* time, on Saturday evening, three days after this (and the conversation can't have occurred during this visit, because this time Weizsäcker was accompanying him.) 'It was in many ways particularly nice,' wrote Heisenberg later that same night. "The conversation turned for a great part of the evening around purely human problems. Bohr read something aloud, I played a Mozart sonata (A major).'

The immediate rupture of the two men's friendship is almost the only aspect of the story which has up to now seemed reasonably unambiguous (I certainly take it for granted in the play). Now even this turns out to be as clouded as everything else.

Rechenberg suggests that it may have been at this farewell meeting that Heisenberg and Weizsäcker urged Bohr to maintain contact with the German Embassy. If so it could have been Bohr's anger at this that colored his recollection of the earlier conversation. It is in any case clear that the quarrel took the form it did only later, in the recollection of the participants, as they reflected upon it - probably also as the circumstances of the war got worse, as the deepest horrors of the Nazi period were uncovered, and as the actual development of nuclear weapons called into question the two men's participation.

History, in other words, is not what happens when it happens, but what seems to people to have happened when they look back upon it.

*

I can't help being moved, by the picture of Bohr drafting and redrafting his letter over the last five years of his life - and still never sending it. He was famous for his endless redrafting of everything he wrote, and here he was trying not only to satisfy his characteristic concern for the precise nuance, but also to reconcile that with his equally characteristic consideration for Heisenberg's feelings. There is a sad parallel with the account which Professor Hans-Peter Dürr gave, at the Heisenberg Centenary symposium in Bamberg, of Heisenberg's rather similar efforts to understand what had happened.

Professor Dürr, who worked for many years with Heisenberg in Göttingen after the war, said that Heisenberg continued to love Bohr to the end of his life, and he recalled his going over the fatal meeting again and again, trying to work out what had happened. Professor Dürr offered what seems to me the most plausible commonsense estimate of Heisenberg's intentions that has yet been advanced. He thought that Heisenberg had simply wanted to have a talk. Heisenberg and Bohr had been so close that they could finish each other's sentences, and he assumed that he would have only to hint at what was on his mind for Bohr to grasp the significance of it. What he had entirely failed to grasp was that the situation had changed, and that Bohr's anger about the German occupation would make the old easy communication entirely impossible.

Whatever was said at the meeting, and whatever Heisenberg's intentions were, there is scmething profoundly characteristic of the difficulties in human relationships, and profoundly painful, in that picture of the two aging men, one in Copenhagen and one in Göttingen, puzzling for all those long years over the few brief moments that had clouded if not ended their friendship. It's what their shades do in my play, of course. At least in the play they get together to work it out.

Overleaf: a diagram outlining the scientific and historical background of the play.

From the beginnings of modern atomic theory to Hiroshima: an outline sketch of the scientific and historical background to the play.

Electrons
1895 Thomson discovers the electron, the extremely light, negatively charged particles orbiting inside the atom which give it its chemical properties.

Quantum Theory
1900 Planck discovers that heat energy is not continuously variable, as classical physics assumes. There is a smallest common coin in the currency, the quantum, and all transactions are in multiples of it.

The Nucleus
1910 Rutherford shows that the electrons orbit around a tiny nucleus, in which almost the entire mass of the atom is concentrated.

Photons
1905 Einstein realizes that light, too, has to be understood not only as waves but as quantum particles, later known as photons.

The Quantum Atom
1913 Bohr realizes that quantum theory applies to matter itself. The orbits of the electrons about the nucleus are limited to a number of separate whole number possibilities, so that the atom can exist only in a number of distinct and definite states. (The incomplete so-called 'old quantum theory'.)

Quantum Mechanics
1925 Heisenberg abandons electron orbits as unobservable, and finds instead a mathematical formulation in terms of matrices for what *can* be observed - the effects they produce upon the absorption and emission of light.

Uncertainty
1927 Heisenberg demonstrates that all statements about the movement of a particle are governed by the uncertainty relationship: the more accurately you know its position, the less accurately you know its velocity, and vice versa.

Matter as Waves
1924 De Broglie in Paris suggests that, just as radiation can be treated as particles, so the particles of matter can be treated as a wave formation.

The Wave Equation
1926 Schrödinger finds the mathematical equation for the wave interpretation, and proves that wave and matrix mechanics are mathematically equivalent.

The Copenhagen Interpretation
1928 Bohr relates the Heisenberg's particle theory and Schrödinger's wave theory by the complementarity principle, according to which the behavior of an electron can be understood completely only by descriptions in both wave and particle form. Uncertainty plus complementarity become established as the pillars of the Copenhagen (or 'orthodox') interpretation of quantum mechanics.

Neutrons
1932 Chadwick discovers the neutron - a particle which can be used to explore the nucleus because it carries no electrical charge, and can penetrate it undeflected.

Into the Nucleus
1932 Heisenberg opens the new era of nuclear physics by using neutron theory to apply quantum mechanics to the structure of the nucleus.

Transmutation
1934 Fermi in Rome bombards uranium with neutrons and produces a radioactive substance which he cannot identify.

Identification
1939 Hahn and Strassmann in Berlin identify the substance produced by Fermi's bombardment as barium, which has only about half the atomic weight of uranium.

The Liquid Drop
1937 Bohr explains the properties of the nucleus by analogy with a drop of liquid.

Fission
1939 Lise Meitner and Frisch in Sweden apply Bohr's liquid drop model to the uranium nucleus, and realize that it has turned into barium under bombardment by splitting into two, with the release of huge quantities of energy.

The Neutrons Multiply
1939 Bohr and Wheeler at Princeton realize that fission also produces free neutrons. These neutrons are moving too fast to fission other nuclei in U-238, the isotope which makes up 99% of natural uranium, and will fission only the nuclei of the U-235 isotope, which constitutes less that 1% of it.

The Chain Reaction
1939 Joliot in Paris and Fermi in New York demonstrate the release of two or more free neutrons with each fission, which proves the possibility of a chain reaction in pure U-235.

The Critical Mass
1940 Frisch and Peierls in Birmingham calculate, wrongly but encouragingly, the minimum amount of U-235 needed to sustain an effective chain reaction.

The War
1939 The Second World War begins, and Germany at once commences research into the military possibilities of fission.

The Manhattan Project
1942 The Allied atomic bomb program begins.

The Reactor
1942 Fermi in Chicago achieves the first self-sustaining chain reaction in a prototype reactor.

Germany Defeated
1945 The Allied advance into Germany halts the atomic program there.

The Bomb
1945 The bomb is successfully tested in July, and in the following month used on Hiroshima.

ANON
Kate Robin

Drama / 2m, 12f / Area

Anon. follows two couples as they cope with sexual addiction. Trip and Allison are young and healthy, but he's more interested in his abnormally large porn collection than in her. While they begin to work through both of their own sexual and relationship hang-ups, Trip's parents are stuck in the roles they've been carving out for years in their dysfunctional marriage. In between scenes with these four characters, 10 different women, members of a support group for those involved with individuals with sex addiction issues, tell their stories in monologues that are alternately funny and harrowing..

In addition to Anon., Robin's play What They Have was also commissioned by South Coast Repertory. Her plays have also been developed at Manhattan Theater Club, Playwrights Horizons, New York Theatre Workshop, The Eugene O'Neill Theater Center's National Playwrights Conference, JAW/West at Portland Center Stage and Ensemble Studio Theatre. Television and film credits include "Six Feet Under" (writer/supervising producer) and "Coming Soon." Robin received the 2003 Princess Grace Statuette for playwriting and is an alumna of New Dramatists.

WHITE BUFFALO
Don Zolidis

Drama / 3m, 2f (plus chorus)/ Unit Set

Based on actual events, WHITE BUFFALO tells the story of the miracle birth of a white buffalo calf on a small farm in southern Wisconsin. When Carol Gelling discovers that one of the buffalo on her farm is born white in color, she thinks nothing more of it than a curiosity. Soon, however, she learns that this is the fulfillment of an ancient prophecy believed by the Sioux to bring peace on earth and unity to all mankind. Her little farm is quickly overwhelmed with religious pilgrims, bringing her into contact with a culture and faith that is wholly unfamiliar to her. When a mysterious businessman offers to buy the calf for two million dollars, Carol is thrown into doubt about whether to profit from the religious beliefs of others or to keep true to a spirituality she knows nothing about.

TREASURE ISLAND
Ken Ludwig

All Groups / Adventure / 10m, 1f (doubling) / Areas

Based on the masterful adventure novel by Robert Louis Stevenson, *Treasure Island* is a stunning yarn of piracy on the tropical seas. It begins at an inn on the Devon coast of England in 1775 and quickly becomes an unforgettable tale of treachery and mayhem featuring a host of legendary swashbucklers including the dangerous Billy Bones (played unforgettably in the movies by Lionel Barrymore), the sinister two-timing Israel Hands, the brassy woman pirate Anne Bonney, and the hideous form of evil incarnate, Blind Pew. At the center of it all are Jim Hawkins, a 14-year-old boy who longs for adventure, and the infamous Long John Silver, who is a complex study of good and evil, perhaps the most famous hero-villain of all time. Silver is an unscrupulous buccaneer-rogue whose greedy quest for gold, coupled with his affection for Jim, cannot help but win the heart of every soul who has ever longed for romance, treasure and adventure.

SKIN DEEP
Jon Lonoff

Comedy / 2m, 2f / Interior Unit Set

In *Skin Deep*, a large, lovable, lonely-heart, named Maureen Mulligan, gives romance one last shot on a blind-date with sweet awkward Joseph Spinelli; she's learned to pepper her speech with jokes to hide insecurities about her weight and appearance, while he's almost dangerously forthright, saying everything that comes to his mind. They both know they're perfect for each other, and in time they come to admit it.

They were set up on the date by Maureen's sister Sheila and her husband Squire, who are having problems of their own: Sheila undergoes a non-stop series of cosmetic surgeries to hang onto the attractive and much-desired Squire, who may or may not have long ago held designs on Maureen, who introduced him to Sheila. With Maureen particularly vulnerable to both hurting and being hurt, the time is ripe for all these unspoken issues to bubble to the surface.

"Warm-hearted comedy ... the laughter was literally show-stopping. A winning play, with enough good-humored laughs and sentiment to keep you smiling from beginning to end."
- TalkinBroadway.com

"It's a little Paddy Chayefsky, a lot Neil Simon and a quick-witted, intelligent voyage into the not-so-tranquil seas of middle-aged love and dating. The dialogue is crackling and hilarious; the plot simple but well-turned; the characters endearing and quirky; and lurking beneath the merriment is so much heartache that you'll stand up and cheer when the unlikely couple makes it to the inevitable final clinch."
- NYTheatreWorld.Com

COCKEYED
William Missouri Downs

Comedy / 3m, 1f / Unit Set

Phil, an average nice guy, is madly in love with the beautiful Sophia. The only problem is that she's unaware of his existence. He tries to introduce himself but she looks right through him. When Phil discovers Sophia has a glass eye, he thinks that might be the problem, but soon realizes that she really can't see him. Perhaps he is caught in a philosophical hyperspace or dualistic reality or perhaps beautiful women are just unaware of nice guys. Armed only with a B.A. in philosophy, Phil sets out to prove his existence and win Sophia's heart. This fast moving farce is the winner of the HotCity Theatre's GreenHouse New Play Festival. The St. Louis Post-Dispatch called Cockeyed a clever romantic comedy, Talkin' Broadway called it "hilarious," while Playback Magazine said that it was "fresh and invigorating."

Winner!
of the HotCity Theatre GreenHouse New Play Festival

"Rocking with laughter...hilarious...polished and engaging work draws heavily on the age-old conventions of farce: improbable situations, exaggerated characters, amazing coincidences, absurd misunderstandings, people hiding in closets and barely missing each other as they run in and out of doors...full of comic momentum as Cockeyed hurtles toward its conclusion."
- Talkin' Broadway

THE OFFICE PLAYS
Two full length plays by Adam Bock

THE RECEPTIONIST
Comedy / 2m, 2f / Interior

At the start of a typical day in the Northeast Office, Beverly deals effortlessly with ringing phones and her colleague's romantic troubles. But the appearance of a charming rep from the Central Office disrupts the friendly routine. And as the true nature of the company's business becomes apparent, The Receptionist raises disquieting, provocative questions about the consequences of complicity with evil.

"...Mr. Bock's poisoned Post-it note of a play."
- New York Times

"Bock's intense initial focus on the routine goes to the heart of *The Receptionist's* pointed, painfully timely allegory... elliptical, provocative play..."
- Time Out New York

THE THUGS
Comedy / 2m, 6f / Interior

The Obie Award winning dark comedy about work, thunder and the mysterious things that are happening on the 9th floor of a big law firm. When a group of temps try to discover the secrets that lurk in the hidden crevices of their workplace, they realize they would rather believe in gossip and rumors than face dangerous realities.

"Bock starts you off giggling, but leaves you with a chill."
- Time Out New York

"... a delightfully paranoid little nightmare that is both more chillingly realistic and pointedly absurd than anything John Grisham ever dreamed up."
- New York Times

CPSIA information can be obtained at www.ICGtesting.com
Printed in the USA
BVOW011137280312

286276BV00011B/3/P

9 780573 627521